EVE: SPIRIT

Tania-Jane

Love you honey XSX

BBF

Tania-Jane!

Published 2008 by arima publishing

ISBN 978 1 84549 351 6

Printed and bound in the United Kingdom

Typeset in Garamond 11

Swirl is an imprint of arima publishing.

arima publishing
ASK House, Northgate Avenue
Bury St Edmunds, Suffolk IP32 6BB
t: (+44) 01284 700321

www.arimapublishing.com

ACKNOWLEDGEMENT

Thank you Cameron for giving me the inspiration to write this and to Elektra-Jade for taking the journey further.

Thank you my husband and best friend Justin for making me continue when I felt like giving in, and for all your hard work. I love you.

Robin and Kerry my sister and friends. Thank you. You made me laugh when I felt like crying. All the nights you stayed up listening to me. I love you both.

Mum and Dad. You gave me my first laptop and helped me more than you think. Love you both.

Paul and Kayleigh, thank you for our chats, I hope they will continue.

To all the people who have been there for me and helped me on this journey, I thank you so much.

Simon Rogers, glad to see you have grown.

Love you all,
Tania-Jane.

The thumping of a heartbeat, the echoes of a strange chanting maybe in Latin, all this noise travelled up from the depths of an old monastery. Every day since the beginning of time even before Christ our saviour was born was leading to this time, tonight and now all over again the birth of something different was about to unfold.

Deep down in the darkness of the eerie echoes, were burning lights, torches of fire in the caves underneath the old monastery. The flames moved around in circles as cloaked hooded men paced around chanting, a red substance, maybe blood poured from a silver chalice, it splashed and rolled over the naked flesh of a young woman, she was gone, her soul was already passed over, but the chanting continued. A main man among the cloaked figures spoke in a louder tone. Her body lay sunken in murky water and around her they praised her heavenly sight, pure and lifeless, she lay with no breath, no pain, for all her sins had long been forgiven. They all longed for her wakening, a wakening to change all the rules, a time for everything unworthy of life to be placed in judgement. This shell of a women the age of about thirty was about to be woken, back from the darkness to carry the sword of our Lord , our God. For all sins men now carry, this burden would be now placed on the shoulders of a woman, but not just any woman. A woman touched from the heavens, lady of strength and justice to all in peril, all working their ways to unborn suffocating religions of darkness and of unearthly sacrifice. This angel would be the love of our Lord, but a different kind than his son Jesus, for she would bring the power of life and death. Once woken her memories of life once gone would come flooding back, but then disappear within hours, days. The people that bring her immortal soul were prepared, they were well aware and read of what would be. The time was now!

THE WAKING

*I could hear, I heard all the echoes of life pulling on me, a waking of pleasure, of pain.
I was drowning in light, beautiful loving light, but now from a distance I felt a calling.
I could hear voices, lost souls screaming in pain and I answered. A whisper of a great
calling spoke into me, and I knew at once of what I must learn, and now do!*

*"I call you my daughter, for now I must place a great choice on your soul, on your
heart. I wish for you to return to a life, your body once broken will be replenished,
restored, you can walk the earth once more, but I have to give you back to the earth for
a price. Daughter of light you will have the strength of an immortal, power of each
element bound to the earth. You speak the power; it will become of what you wish,
against the dark powers on earth now. I will be with your every step until you take
flight on your own path to search and destroy the evil that now walks amongst all
earth's creatures. Your price is high to say this; it will be hard for you. For now when
you return memories will become clear of whom you once were, but you will start to
forget, you must. To hold on to such feelings could prevent the tasks you must take; you
cannot look back my daughter, only forward. I ask a lot from your bounded soul. Will
you take the sword of justice, or stay among the frosted glass of light?"*

*"I know what you ask, and I feel them calling, I know it will be very hard and of the
struggles I must face. I could feel my place here is love, but back in the living realms I
am needed. I will go my Lord, back to the living; I will pledge my light for you."*

*I felt no words come from my mouth, my lips, but I heard what I spoke deep down
within, and so did my God!*

The change of mood happened dramatically from the chanting rhythms
and motions, to the silence and stillness all around, even in the air itself.
No echoes, nothing. A smell of earth and flowers filled the air as the main
man of the cloaked figures stood over the hollow and the young woman.
The man pushed back his cloak hood and stood tall on the rock altar; his
face was very stern, he was a wise man of about fifty, with little hair. He
was slender and captivating.

"Awake our daughter, child of light, we pray of thee, we ask of thee, to
show your light, your power. Oh child lost in darkness, hear our cries,
awake from your eternal sleep, and bring your divine power and wisdom
with you, for you are the chosen." He shouts this for all to hear and slices
his hand, as he does the knife brings blood and life as it spills into the
murky water and the man switches off from the pain.

"Take your breath and return, we ask of thee, to take judgement on this
cruel and horrific realm. Breathe and be! We bid your blood to run, to
awake your soul. Angel of light, come back to us, resurrect your shell!"

He gazes below him, into the water, and then reaches far to the top of the cave, his voice now slightly trembling from the flow of blood, he screams out. "Lord our God, it is time. The beast is becoming stronger. AWAKE HER SOUL!"

One of the cloaked figures pulled back his hood and knelt down to the waters edge. "The water! It's becoming clearer, nearly crystal clear, and it feels... it feels warms" He is a young man of about twenty-five; he sounds grateful and slightly excited.

Everyone now watches in silence as the water clears, and as it does her bodies' wounds begin to heal. The man on the altar opens up his fist in amazement. His wound is healing too.

It is true, and they all knew it was starting to happen. Life!

It all began at once; the light grew so bright; it felt too intense to be part of it. I saw images in front of me, moving with great speed. It was like watching a film on rewind as everything seemed to be going backwards.

It stopped. Everything stopped. All was still and the light faded; then the darkness grew all around me once more. Again like a sudden snap, there was light all around me, but this time the images were playing forward and in a way I understood. Now they jumped from one scene to another. I recognised the images before me, it was my life, or at least the one I used to belong to. I see my mother; she is so beautiful as she sings to me, and there is my father sat by us reading the newspaper. It feels so great to see them once more. Then I see myself as a toddler, chasing our dog. I see my family at my eighteenth birthday party. I see my friends at high school playing netball, my old jobs, many people and places, things I had forgotten I had done. I see myself at a wedding, it's my wedding, and there's my husband. I look on to the birth of our son, he is so gorgeous, and I have missed them all so much.

Now I see a busy road, I'm there at the road, holding on to my son so tightly, the lights changed to green and he pulls away from me. I shout at him to be careful. Looking up and down the road I see a speeding car it's getting closer and it's not slowing down. They don't see my little boy, I run, and I push him onto the grass on the other side of the road. I remember the pain as it hits my mortal body, so hard for so long. I tried to stay alive, to breathe. I remember the rushing, and confusing feelings as my husband let me go in peace. They tried hard to save me.

The last words I remember were "Time of death on the twenty-first of April two thousand and three, nine twenty-five a.m."

This I now see before me was gone and I had to forget, none of it could or should matter anymore but deep inside me it did. Even though I knew I would forget my heart would hold the truth.

The fresh image of the impact of the accident hit me again. I sprung up with a loud deep gasp for air. Water splashed around my body and cloaked figures stared. My eyes were wide and open; my body naked and cold. The feelings of life itself rushed into my soul, and I breathed once more. I was awake!

I heard a roar, a voice screaming out into the air. I felt pain and relief as I took air and life back into my lungs, my body. My eyes seemed blurred like a newborn baby as I tried to fix them onto anything that made movement. I felt my muscles aching in every part of my body. Feeling with my fingertips, I felt my stomach and tried to focus. Deep inside me my body structure was changing, I was healing, and more. Definition, my body felt toned, and I felt so pure, so alive. I knew the scream I heard was from me, from the energy that roared and grew within me. A voice grew louder from the distance, my head was still taking everything in, and absorbing what was necessary to everything I needed.

"You're here, you're here, and you are beautiful. Can you hear me child?"

A male figure stood before the naked woman and a plump woman pushed him aside. "Let me see this soul, err you'll want this my love". The gentle woman wrapped a grey soft blanket around her back as she sat in the water.

The Soul raised her arms and hands from the hollow and tried to push herself up onto the rock and dirt that surrounded her, the water swirled around her knees as she rested herself on the surface above. She crawled from the water and felt the rough of the rock and dirt on her knees as she tried to rise up on to her feet. Two men held her arms as she tried to stand. She still felt too weak, and she pushed them aside as best she could. She groaned but said nothing as she fell back to her knees.

The Soul looked down towards the floor where two feet stood just before her.

"Stand my child stand, you must forget the past be strong, remember your strength, you know why you are here and everything to be done. "STAND!" The man glared into her eyes as she grabbed the air and screamed into him.

She was standing, she stood looking around as for the first time, she could see. The man in front of her seemed to know her fears, his face looked stern, he was unafraid. This man brought her back to save a world filled with fears of ignorance.

Another young woman approached her and handed her a dark gown. "Thank you". It was the first time she had spoken. The woman looked surprised and the man in front smiled.

THE BEGINNING

Feelings of uncertainties filled the reborn soul, was this her new family?
Would she ever feel she would belong? Would that ever matter? She
knew of what her ventures would be and what new paths would unravel.
Time would make her; break her into what she would now hold dear to
her heart; freedom and love. The fires of evil will have to all be burnt out,
and it was her and her leadership that would bring that day to come.

'The Soul pulled the gown over her body and pondered on what to ask.
There was still much more she wanted to learn; why me? All the millions
of people and creatures on this earth that die every day, why choose me?
Deep inside her she already knew.
A hand touched her shoulder, "I suppose there is a lot you want to
understand? My name is Father Josh; I will be your support and servant. I
will always be your friend and try to lead you to the right paths child."
Father Josh walked beside her and touched her hand, he felt warm and
kind. As he touched her hand something happened to her that was all too
much; that she was not ready to take in.
'The Soul saw him, his life, and his pain, all that he had ever felt. She saw
his wife fall to her death, she saw the men that took her life, the way they
laughed at him as he lay trapped under gravel in his car. His pain was
inside her turning and twisting; it was pulling in her heart ; a frustrating
feeling of being helpless to do anything. Suddenly she was within the cave
once again, she had her head in her hands; it was all too much.
Father Josh was looking at 'The Soul, his eyes were glazed over, but he
was holding onto the tears.
"I don't know if I want that gift." She said as she stood back on her feet.
"Is this for keeping, did you see it too?" 'The Soul asked Father Josh as
she took her hands away from her eyes.
"I saw... I saw it and felt it too. It's ok, you will learn to use it, like the
rest of your gifts it will come together. You need to rest, in the morning
things will have settled." Father Josh sounded so certain in all his words;
she trusted everything he had spoken.
"When morning arrives my memories will be more images that fade. I do
understand why I am here tonight, but Father I just can't understand,
why me?" She asked a posing question, everyone in the cave seemed to
understand why she asked.
"You gave your mortal life for another, without hesitation, without fear.
It made you pure without sin. Everything you have chosen to do even
before that has led you here. Even the silly things; your body art, three

symbols placed onto your body, they all symbolised prosperity. They will fade just like your memories, but your heart is strong." Father Josh smiled, he seemed happy. She felt like she was the daughter he always wanted. This was her new family and they understood each other.

As she looked around at the different faces before her she sensed something stirring, the feelings of hatred and force were in the air, not quite here, but soon. Someone or something approached; a forceful feeling was creeping up on them.

The two women attended her side as she sat down on a rock. "Are you ready to move on from here my love?" the plump lady asked sounding concerned for the just woken soul.

"I'm not quite ready yet, I feel a presence getting close to us" she said as she looked up into their faces. It might have sounded strange to anyone who didn't know this situation, but it was clear something was wrong. "What are your names?"

"Our names... I am Sister Vern, and this young lady beside me is Kate, she was a homeless child I took under my wing."

She looked at Vern as she spoke; she tried to distract herself from the growing feeling approaching. She tried to guess Vern's age in her head. Vern looked about forty-three, probably a widow or spinster; she had a kind face and blossomed with confidence. Kate looked worn, she was quite pretty and slim, but she looked like she took a back seat in everything and just followed along, afraid to be alone. Kate's body language was unsteady; she had worries on her mind.

All of a sudden she could hear a change in pitch from up above them. Nobody else seemed to be aware of anything different at all; they were clearing away the candles and throwing the torches into the hollow.

"Shh, be still, I hear someone, voices, someone approaches and it doesn't feel good," one by one everyone stood still to listen.

BANG, BANG, BANG!

"Josh... Vern, we know you are down there, there is no escaping. You can't bring her back; Lucas is too strong for you, LET US IN!" The doors blew off their hinges, she could hear them bash against something, and then there were footsteps running down some steps.

A panicked look was in Kate's eyes; the others seemed to be only slightly concerned. The deed was already done why should they worry?

Father Josh had a proud and firm expression on his face, as they began to appear in front of them from the doorway of the spiralled stone steps.

"You are too late, she is already here among us now, and she is ready for you and your unworthy threats." Father Josh never moved his eyes from the man that stood in front of him.

There were six men all together, the main man among them looked about forty; he was tall and had shoulder length grey hair. The other men looked roughly around the age of twenty-five to thirty and they looked like they were about to go into battle. All dressed in jeans and dark jackets it looked like an old biker gang missing their bikes. The Soul didn't know whether to feel threatened or flattered.

The Soul stood forward and looked at the man; he turned and looked at her; up and down carefully studying her form. "What?! Do you think I will not take your life once more?" He looked at her with vengeance as he spoke, like he already knew of what was to come. His tactics didn't bother her, he could try to use control, but this was just a tactic to try and talk her down like she was nothing.

The Soul took a long breath and spoke into the cave, "Everyone that wants to still walk this realm stand behind me, if you want to live that is!" Movement filled the room as the sides were taken to who would stand and who would fall. Behind her stood her party of life bringers and in front of her stood an army that made them all feel deep darkness.

"Well this is where it ends, we will prevail and you will be crushed. I mean look at her, why choose a woman? What will you do slap me?" He chuckled loud as he spoke, and The Soul felt like she had already won as his thoughts had already betrayed him and his followers.

"You're right I am a woman, a woman is where all life begins. But you are wrong, it won't end here. This is just the beginning for me and of it all." As she spoke her face tensed.

The man pulled his right hand out from under his long leather jacket, the sword he made emerge glimmered slightly in the dim light. The Soul felt no fear, our Lord himself had already told her of his protection. Until she has taken her first flight, this fight was to be over before it could begin.

The man raised the sword high into the air and as he did she raised her arms at shoulder height. A ring of light surfaced from the floor; it seemed like minutes but it only took seconds to sweep in front of them. The light surrounded the other men, screams were heard and thumps, and then a dazzling bright flash of light filled the cave then disappeared. A smoky air was left with nothing more but the remains of just ash and stone on the floor. This was the power, a gift, but she had not made this happen this time, this was the 'Lord of Light' watching over her soul.

All who stood with her; all who stood behind were hidden with her protection. It was no contest. Defeated by their own mistakes the twisted souls before them were no more.

Father Josh scattered the ashes with his feet, he looked at all present and then 'The Soul. He faced all with confidence. He claimed only what they all thought, and what she knew. "So it begins".

A calm feeling filled 'The Soul as they walked away from the old monastery; the remains of such a beautiful old building. The structure was broken, but the comfort and peaceful air was still present. She looked back at the old remains that were her birthplace as she sat down in the back seat of a travel cruiser.

As she adjusted the seat belt she thought maybe this would be the last time she would see this place. As the engine started it occurred to her she didn't even know where she was or what day on earth they were in. It triggered emotions from her death and the last words she had heard. How long had her body laid still for?

Martin was the man who was driving this eight-seated cruiser. He seemed young, but his age she guessed was about thirty, well that's still young in many ways for anyone to witness what had happened this evening. Quietness filled the cruiser as they travelled back onto the open road and she wasn't ready to sit and be silent. 'The Soul had many questions filling her head and she really needed answers.

Travelling behind them were two more cars that joined their ongoing unit of believers. She could see the speed at which they travelled from where she sat. They were travelling steady and easy, no point in rushing. She turned to Vern who sat beside her, she needed to find some answers; it was driving her crazy having all these new ideas and questions inside her.

"Vern I need to know some details, please just answer no matter if you think it will shock me. What is the date... the year, and where are we going?" As she spoke, Vern traced the outline of her face in the dark; she stared into 'The Soul for a few seconds then softly began to speak.

"Well my love we should have spoken before we left, but, well things sort of moved on quite quickly. The date is the thirty-first of July, two thousand and ten and we are travelling towards England. Ok love?"

"Yes that's about what I thought, but where are we at this moment? Because unless things have really been out of sorts we seem to be driving on the wrong side of this road and I'm sure we can't be in the UK." 'The

Souls question seemed to amuse Sister Vern and the other passengers as a couple of snorts and chuckles filled the air.

"Erm, well we are passing trough France at the moment and have just left Cîteaux. We will be stopping over in London then our journey will go on to Ireland, but as for you only you will know your own journey."

The Soul understood Sister Vern's wise words. Her journey from England and her duties would be her own, and she knew she would need no signs to find her way. Lucas and his demons would find her, but it was no waiting game, she will have to be always one step ahead. At this moment these people beside her would be her only help until she finds her disciples.

They must have been travelling for about thirty minutes into their long journey. Martin pulled up in front of an old public house, Vern was resting; her light breath could be heard as she slept. Martin placed his hand onto Kate's knee then turned to face The Soul as they stopped.

"This is where we are resting tonight, got an early start back to England tomorrow," his voice was soft and caring. The Soul realised she was probably the only one who knew of the love between these two persons before her.

Kate pushed Martins hand away and looked at The Soul; she smiled and gave Kate reassuring eyes.

"So what time are we leaving?"

"Well I suppose it's really today in about five and a half hours. Sorry not must rest hey? But you have been getting a lot of rest lately". Martin amused himself with his humour and The Soul just smiled thinking what he witnessed tonight could distract anyone from reality, and emotions deliver themselves in strange unattached behaviour.

Kate grabbed a bag from the back of the cruiser as The Soul gently disturbed Vern to wake. "Oh what is the time love?"

The Soul looked at the vehicles' luminous clock, "It's twelve forty-three a.m. Vern, and we have arrived at our resting place."

The building was quite dimly lit; a silhouette of a male figure stood at the doorway, Father Josh approached him and they both faded into the entrance of the old building. As they all walked through the building people sat at their tables still drinking and giggling into the night air. Some people stared and others regardless carried on with their evening chatter, the night for them was still young.

'Harbour Inn' the sign read on the door as they made their way to the back of the bar. The noise from the bar seemed to drift off as they made their way up the flight of stairs. 'The Soul was starting to feel so tired; these few hours had been quite tiresome on her mental being.

Father Josh stood beside her and told her she would be sharing a room with Kate and Sister Vern, it was nice for her to know she wouldn't be alone with her thoughts and feelings tonight. They all looked quite drained and all said little to each other, so 'The Soul left her questions for the morning when their brains would be more refreshed…

Kate lay in her bed looking towards the ceiling she whispered soft to herself as Sister Vern pottered around the room getting things sorted for the morning journey. As 'The Soul lay still in the darkness wrapped up in a heavy blanket she pondered on what the guests at the bar must have thought to all of them turning up. They all looked like a Halloween tribute and they all seemed to be on their guard. She lay and listened to the voices below as she fell to sleep.

THE NEW JOURNEY

'The Soul stirred to the early chatter of birds singing out to one another. She quickly sat up in bed and the realisation settled back in of who she was and why she was back in the living realm.

Vern and Kate were still resting but she could hear that Vern was beginning to stir. A rattle on the door made Kate jump up suddenly.

"It's Martin, time to start getting things together for the journey. It's five thirty, looks like it's going to be a nice day."

"Ok be with you shortly, we are just getting dressed." Vern replied.

'The Soul drew back the curtains and opened the window; the air smelt fresh and the light began to break away through the dark clouds, it felt like a good morning to her.

"Here these are for you, hope they are ok?" Kate asked as she passed some blue jeans and a black t-shirt to 'The Soul. "I have a jacket too if you want it, we can go shopping when we get to England if you like?"

"Yes, thanks that's so nice, I like them, my size too" she said as she tried on the jacket.

Kate looked pleased with herself and happy; she liked them.

"Why don't you take a shower love in the en-suite – we have time; get freshened up. You will feel much better." Vern looked at 'The Soul knowing she felt a bit murky and needed to cleanse her body.

"Yes I will, I won't be long, I promise" she grabbed the towel that hung over the chair by the window and walked towards the bathroom.

'The Soul could hear everybody stirring and talking as she walked passed the bedroom door.

As she stepped from the shower she caught a slight reflection of herself in the mirror on the back of the door. She wanted to see herself and swallowed hard and cleared the steam with her hand for a reflection. "This is me" she told herself.

Her hair was golden brown, down past her shoulders with a slight curl. She looked much more toned; even her stomach muscles were more pronounced than she remembered. Her eyes a piercing green and she still looked young. She looked the same in many ways to how she used to be, but there were definite changes. Would anybody she used to know recognise her? It didn't really matter now because she would never meet anyone she used to know would she.

Everybody soon gathered stuff together and walked down to the bar, the manager was there to greet them. He offered everyone breakfast, but

Father Josh told him they were too busy, "we really have to go", the man understood and shook Josh's hand.

As they walked towards the vehicles 'The Soul felt the air change just like before. She knew that someone approached them, but whom? In that moment she had a vision, her mind went blank and then there was a bright light. She saw what was approaching, two men on motorbikes, they had been sent by Lucas. Not to kill, but to bring a message and to try and take one of them... Kate. 'The Soul opened her eyes and looked around, no one to be seen yet, but they were on their way she could hear their bikes in the distance and they wouldn't out run them.

"Josh, Lucas has sent two men, they will be here soon, and they want to take Kate."

Father Josh looked at Kate with annoyed eyes. "What have you done, WHAT HAVE YOU DONE?!"

Hysterically Kate started jabbering and fell on to the floor scared and crying.

"Help me please... Please! I couldn't help it, I couldn't stop it, and he made me."

"What is it Kate, tell me. I will stop this, but you must tell me" 'The Soul tried to understand, but she was too hysterical,

"Take my hand Kate, show me what has happened." Kate looked into 'The Soul's eyes as she took her hand.

In a big flash of light 'The Soul saw through her eyes and heard through her ears. Kate was desperate to trace her family, Martin had made her pregnant, she felt confused and alone and Lucas had come to her. Lucas told her Sister Vern and Father Josh would banish her and make her get rid of her unborn baby, Lucas said he could help. He would make her lose the baby naturally and take her to her family for a price. Kate had to tell him the details of the times and places of 'The Soul's rebirth and where they would stay and if it fell through Kate would belong to him. Kate had agreed, and now because her information had not brought Lucas justice she would now have to bow down to him.

Kate had lost her baby when Lucas forced himself on her, he raped her and she bled. Lucas's strength was too much for her confused mind, so she told him what she could and he healed her body and let her go, knowing still her bargain was made Kate knew Lucas would soon come to collect her life. Martin doesn't know, but Kate felt trapped; if she told him she might lose him, but if she doesn't he will find out soon and she will lose him anyway.

'The Soul felt Kate's inner turmoil and fear of now, but 'The Soul would not let Lucas take her, Lucas would have to go through 'The Soul first, and she was ready.

As 'The Soul let go of Kate's hands she held her close and whispered in her ear. "It's ok, let me deal with this, I will not let him take you, trust me."

Kate was now standing and Sister Vern held her in her arms.

"Martin, take her to the car I will speak to her soon!" Father Josh sounded anxious. He turned to Vern. "Go with them!" he ordered.

"What did you see? I need to know if we can trust her." He wanted some comfort in the words he was about to hear.

"I will tell you on the journey, we can trust her... She just fell for a while, but Kate will be ok." 'The Soul tried to reassure him, but Father Josh still wanted answers.

The bikes got closer and 'The Soul had no intentions of running, she wanted to make sure Lucas knew she was here and she was in no mood to play games.

The two bikes roared up onto the dirt road and the bikers roared the engines before turning them off. One red bike and one black; fast racing bikes, chunky and filled with power. The bikers dismounted and took off their helmets and as they did 'The Soul stood tall waiting for their words.

"We have come for the girl."

"I know why you are here and you can't have her, so why don't you just get back on your bikes and tell Lucas he will have to go through me first." They looked astonished and looked at each other, 'The Soul looked at their form; both tall, one slim, one broad with short dark hair, both were about five foot ten inches she guessed. They looked directly at her and the chunky male spoke.

"Ok, so what's your name? I will tell him after we have finished with you and the rest."

"He knows who I am, so let's get this over with," she cunningly grinned. Suddenly the big one came running up at her, gritting his teeth and bringing his crash helmet up into the air, she ducked down low to the ground. As he fell over the top of her she grabbed his crash helmet. The thinner man strode up to her and swung for her face, she blocked his punch with her left arm and kicked him straight in the groin, and as he held his crotch and fell to the floor she kneed him in the face.

The bigger man stood back up and grabbed her leg. She fell back onto the dirt and turned over to stop his heavy boot stomping on her. She sprung back to her feet, he growled at her and helped his friend back up; they breathed heavily and looked bent with rage.

"Come on let's see what you really have!" their words were filled with anger.

The slim male ran back to his bike and grabbed a metal bar.

"Let's go," he said.

"Ok" she said willingly.

They came running towards her and as they did she kicked the bigger male in the face, it made him trip to the left side of her. She raised her right arm to the sky and blocked the thinner man's metal bar from hitting her skull. He came at her again, but this time she kicked him in the stomach and he fell to the floor.

She held her arms in front of her and shouted, "Air protect me!"

The wind picked up; she felt the energy within her ready for her commands. 'The Soul shouted, "fire protect me!" She felt her body grow warmer and her fingers tingle.

The men stood before her again, and as they came at her she raised her right arm towards them, pushing out at the air. She hollered out as a force of air pounded out hitting the slim guy, knocking him ten feet backwards. She pushed her left arm out and another force of air knocked the bigger guy backwards.

Winded they tried to get on their bikes to run her down. The bikes started and roared. They spun around in the dirt and headed towards her. She pushed her right arm out and from her hand; a ball of air and fire flew through the air and hit the big male's bike. It smashed and broke up into flames with a big bang.

'The Soul heard Kate scream out as she witnessed the destruction and heard the big guys' moan as he turned to ash. The thin guy spun his bike around in fear and made a run for it. 'The Soul left him; she let him go to spread the word, to tell Lucas she was ready.

'The Soul felt the release of energies leave her body as she walked back to the cars. Father Josh was still standing outside the travel cruiser his face remained stern. She could read his emotions, he was still in a state of frustration with Kate and he looked at 'The Soul for answers.

'The Soul knew the truth would have to be told as she climbed into the cruiser and Father Josh followed. Sister Vern passed 'The Soul a bottle of water, it tasted so good as she swallowed, and it refreshed her taste buds and took away the thirst she'd had for so long.

"Let's get out of here, we need to be moving now, we can talk on he way" Father Josh explained as he tapped the drivers seat. He turned to face 'The Soul as she sat behind him; Vern and Kate huddled together beside her. Kate was still sobbing.

"I'm so sorry Father... Sister Vern please forgive me, I have been so confused and done wrong...Please."

Kate wanted to hear their words of forgiveness so desperately, she held her hand out towards Josh, and he looked down to the floor and then touched her fingertips.

"Please tell me what I should forgive then we will decide what we can do" Father Josh explained.

"Kate made a mistake." 'The Soul tried to make some understanding for Father Josh.

"Kate you must tell them, because when you become so weak this is when you need them most, Lucas and the others will only pray on your fears you must now be truthful." She looked at her with deep compassion.

Thank you so much for saving me, thank you." Kate began to cry again.

"They will be back you know, but next time you will be ready and much stronger" 'The Soul explained to her.

"Explain child and we will listen." Father Josh told Kate with reassuring eyes.

"Father I was confused, Martin needs to know too. I got lost for a while; Lucas promised to take me to my family he said he could help."

Martin slowed down the car, to listen to her pain but hers would soon be his, so 'The Soul insisted he should stop the car. Father Josh seemed to understand so he told Darrel to drive.

Darrel followed Father Josh everywhere he went, a main candidate to take his place if anything unexpected should ever happen, he was very good looking, dark hair and nicely posed but a man of few words so far.

Darrel took over the wheel, and Martin stepped into the back of the car looking very concerned, and took Kate's hand. Kate explained what happened as they travelled on. The pain of her grief shook the emotions of them all, but they knew there would be more to come; not from this now but from other episodes of this war we are all in. The future would bring more trials but also more hope; for 'The Soul would stand and fight for good... for love... for all of us.

As they travelled on, the truth was out and as Martin comforted Kate stillness filled the car once more. Thinking now from the start 'The Soul realised Kate had something on her mind, her fears that showed from the beginning from when they first met, but now the puzzle was together. Kate was safe once more and free from her torment for now.

"Darrel please switch the radio on we need some reality back here." 'The Soul tried to bring a smile to the faces before her as she spoke.

Darrel did as she asked, Sister Vern tried to smile, Kate looked at Martin with loving eyes and Father Josh turned to 'The Soul once more.

"Yes you're right, we need to get back from pondering on what's happened and focus on now." Father Josh spoke to them all.

Ironically the song playing sounded like someone having a joke as the lyrics spilled from the radio. "People try to take my soul away... But they don't hear the music that I play, Crazy... Crazy... Crazy nights."

'The Soul remembered the song but couldn't place who sang it or where she had heard it, but it didn't matter, it brought life back into the car.

As they approached the docks of France, Darrel parked the cruiser at a café, the smell of salt air was everywhere, and 'The Soul could taste it as they walked towards the café doorway.

"We need to sit down and discuss your papers; you have to have some sort of proof before we travel on. I have a passport; a new name for you, a date of birth and address." Darrel handed them to 'The Soul as she sat down at a six-seated table against the front window.

"See more than just a pretty face," he teased.

"Good work back there, didn't expect Kate and Martin to come clean, poor guys." Darrel obviously had suspected for a while.

"Yes, they will be ok. So you're American and a brain teaser; a whiz with hacking I see." 'The Soul said luring him away from the elements of what had happened today.

She looked at the passport as Father Josh sat down with Vern in front of her.

"Eve... we named you Eve. I hope you don't mind it's just that Eve was the first woman to walk the earth in the good book. I know it's only a story, but now for you it's well justified." Father Josh's eyes swirled with hope and wonder.

"Yes, that's fine, absolutely fine, I like it. I guess it didn't seem right to start addressing me as someone else so soon after I woke from the past. Now feels right." She studied her passport for a moment while Father Josh and the others ordered food and drink.

"What would you like?" Darrel asked posing the menu under Eve's nose.

"Some coffee would be great, oh and maybe some toast, thank you." Eve handed the waitress the menu as she took a note on her pad and walked away.

'The Soul's new name was Eve Honey Mellifont, her birthday was the thirty-first of January, nineteen seventy-seven. Seven years had passed by since her death and her age hadn't changed. Her address she would have to memorise a bit longer, Rock Street, Boyle Town in Ireland.

They all walked from the café and as they did Eve took a deep breath inwards.

"I love that smell, the smell of the sea. It's life." Eve smiled and looked at the others behind her as they stepped on board the boat to take them to England. She decided to take some time to herself on board; she found a nice hide-away on deck to relax and meditate on her own. The sun was now shining brightly, and the water lapped against the sides as they sailed smoothly over the seas.

The boat docked in the afternoon; the sun was still a new gleaming bright glow and it was such a beautiful day, you could just drift away from the war that was all around, but still hidden.

A hand touched Eve's shoulder as she looked over the edge of the railings.

"Come on Eve it's time to go. There are a few people you need to meet."

"Who would they be?" Eve asked as she gripped on to the rails that were along the dock.

"Some friends who can help you with some skills and they are believers too." Father Josh sounded like he was mocking her a little, but she understood, because would anyone be able to believe what they had brought forth?

"The book of Enoch and the scripts, do they have them? I would like to read from the scripts – to know the details of what has been and gone."

"Yes they have copies; the originals are in safe places."

Father... FATHER! Josh!" A voice from a crowd called out to greet them as Darrel pulled up in the travel cruiser.

"Hi there, glad you made it."

"Hi Astra, it's been an eventful day already. This is Eve, and she is learning very quickly." Father Josh kissed Astra's cheek; she then shook Eve's hand with great delight.

"This is so cool, you really are here. I have so much to show you and there are more to help."

Astra was blonde and slim, nice looking. You could tell she was a delight to be around, but she took no attitude from anyone.

"Hello Astra, I'm pleased to meet a new friend of this extended family."

Astra chuckled, "Yes, I know what you mean, we just keep growing."

"Finished talking Astra? We need to get going, things to do!" Darrel revved the engine.

"Screw you Darrel! We're coming." Astra joked back at Darrel.

You could tell they were friends; it was obvious they had spent a lot of time together and knew their boundaries.

"Come on you two we have a guest, I'm sure she will get to know you both well. Act like adults, for now hey!" Josh seemed amused but direct with his approach to their probable long standing debates.

"Hi guys, are we all here? Yes? Great…"

Everyone turned to look at Kate and Martin. At last they were free with their relationship and held each other close.

"Looks like someone's had fun, what have you been up to?" Astra mocked.

"That's enough of that Astra, come on it's time to go." Father Josh stopped the mocking before it began, Astra had not witnessed what had happened this morning, but she would soon learn what had unfolded.

"Ah, the docks of London, what a sight! It's time to have your papers at hand folks." Darrel stopped the car; he lowered the window for the security officer.

"Hi there, how many of you then? Have you got anything to declare?" A chubby short man looked around the vehicle as he asked his questions, then his eyes made contact with Darrel again.

"Nothing to declare here, there are seven of us present and two more cars behind us." Father Josh lent across Darrel as he spoke to the security officer through the window.

"Ok mate lets just see your passports then. My mate here with his dog is just going to have a look around the vehicle; we just have to be safe." A strong looking man stood with the hound.

"Fine mate, yes when you're ready, they can go." The strong looking man nodded.

"Have a safe journey, goodbye." He held his hand into the air as they passed.

Darrel pulled off onto a sidetrack to wait for the rest of the convoy, and soon there were all on their way into the city.

"So I was wondering Eve do you actually remember anything from the past?" Astra sat next to Eve; her blue eyes filled with wonder.

"I don't remember anything much, I remember my son's name and little things that's all. I remember his smell but everything else is just a daze. It isn't like I don't know anything; I mean I'm not starting from scratch. I know names of places and where things are but I can't relate times or where I know anything. I know even my memories of my son's name will fade soon. I have to forget my past life or it could endanger everyone that matters in this turmoil."

Astra looked at her with a sense of sadness, but deep inside she knew that the past is the past and Eve had to bring righteousness back to the future. Darrel stared at Eve for a while using the rear view mirror, he understood as did they all. If she let herself slip just once it could kill them all and she was glad to forget because when she was resurrected she wanted nothing more than to hold her baby in her arms and to tell her husband Jake she loved him. Her past was gone and so had her pain.

A NEW TEACHING

They arrived in London and the chaos of the London traffic hadn't changed much in the last few years. The busy sounds and people rushing around made Eve suddenly realise the reality of now.

"We are here!" Darrel pointed towards a building that looked like an old youth centre that had been refurbished.

The building had a double wooden door in the centre and two large rectangle windows either side. 'Temple of Life' the sign read above the door; the detached building was centred between two shops and a flower stall was outside on the pavement.

"You can jump out here and I'll park up round the back." Darrel said.

Eve guessed they were not far from the city centre; she could hear the hustle and bustle of the streets from where she stood on the step outside 'Temple of Life'. She pushed open the left side of the double doors and stepped into the dimly lit hallway. The floor was a shiny warm marble effect with a bamboo mat that stretched from the front entrance right to the back of the hall.

As she walked inside and up the hall Astra and the others followed. Astra stepped in front of the others and turned to Eve.

"I can show you around now if you like. It's ok it won't take long." She grinned as she took Eve's arm.

Every door was in double; it looked strong and more expressive, Eve and Astra took the first door on the left and Astra turned to face Eve as they stood in the middle of the room.

"This room you see here takes up the whole side of this building."

"This is impressive, this is great! All this equipment is for training – for fighting and meditation, right?" Eve suggested.

"Yes, that's right. Jin-Joel is the master here and he is pretty cute. We have punch bags and pads; we have weights, ropes and meditation techniques. Jin-Joel will show you the rest, I'm sure you will enjoy his teachings; he has some other techniques and skills to teach you too."

"With weapons?" Eve sounded sure.

"Yes, umm, you're right on top aren't you?"

"Got to be right!" Eve said with a smirk as she looked around for further detail in the room.

It was fairly big, with equipment laid spaciously around. There was even a fighting ring at the back of the room; this place was ready for action and she couldn't wait to meet Jin-Joel.

As they both turned to leave, the door opened and an oriental looking man approached them. He looked relaxed and the calmness seemed to follow him inside. He was nice looking and looked like he was in his late thirties, but you couldn't really guess.

"Hello, you must be Eve, I am so happy to be meeting you; this is such an opportunity to be able to help you and teach you some more skills." He lowered his body in her presence and his eyes were filled with great respect. She watched his body move under his robe and noticed his toned figure; she knew he was dedicated to his life and his temple.

"Thank you Jin-Joel it is a great honour for me to be here and to meet someone who shares the fight to stand by my side." Eve bowed herself in his honour and she felt admiration and the greatest respect.

Watching them in the doorway were Father Josh and Darrel, they said nothing but looked on as Eve and Astra walked towards them.

"I will expect to see you first thing in the morning then Eve! Six a.m. wake up call, will meet you here." Jin-Joel smiled at her and she could say nothing to this determined figure as she turned back to face the others.

"Well let's get you settled in then." Darrel pulled a big bag onto his left shoulder and looked at Eve with suggestive eyes to follow him.

They all walked into the room that was opposite, it was a nice study room filled with books, and there also stood an old globe of the world on the desk beside the door on the left. On the left and in front was a bookcase and a laptop computer, which was lying shut on the desk. Next to it was a book open on the pages of 'Fallen Angels'.

Eve looked at everyone as they all stood in the room; Darrel and Father Josh moved towards the left centred bookcase and moved it slightly away from the wall. They didn't have to push it too far before it revealed a staircase that headed down into a dim light.

"So this is how you get your kicks Darrel, luring girls into the darkness." Eve smiled.

"Sorry, I really have to fix this doorway, OWWW!" Darrel mocked as he blundered into the darkness.

"Ah, lights!" Astra sighed as she flicked a switch to the right side of the doorway.

The metal tapped in rhythms to their feet as they all walked down into the living area.

"This is it honey, this is where we all hang out, where we live and work." Darrel threw the bag onto the floor and then dropped himself onto the brown leather sofa in front of him.

"So it's myself, Astra and you all in the same space. Well I don't mind Astra but a male ego, come on!" Eve looked at Darrel with a big smile as he threw a black cushion at her.

"Come on now go and get yourself settled in, Astra will show you around." Father Josh looked a bit concerned with the entertainment as he urged Eve to get herself together.

The sitting room was not too big, but comfortable for four or five people. There was a leather sofa and chair and a square glass coffee table in the middle. A television was against the wall under the staircase. The kitchen was to the right of the sitting room; on the left it was all open planned. The kitchen was white with a lot of lighting and glass panels. As the girls walked passed the kitchen Astra pointed out the bathroom that was beside it; the last door on the right. Facing the kitchen were three doors, the first was Darrel's bedroom, the second Astra's and the last was now Eve's, and it was facing the bathroom door.

"This I think will be perfect." Eve claimed as she pushed open her new bedroom door.

Kate walked in with them and sat on the double bed, "I'm going to miss you Eve; I know we have not known each other long, but you have made my life seem free, and you have saved me from myself." She stared down to the floor then back at Eve with glazed eyes.

"Don't be stupid, oh Kate we will see each other again, a lot, I'm sure. I will always be here when you need me you know that." Eve knelt down and grabbed her wrists reassuringly.

Eve's new bedroom was a dusky rose colour. It had thick cream covers on the bed and long cream curtains at the tall windows on the right of the room. The bed was centred behind the door facing the other windows, bringing in the bright light of day.

"Could I have some time with Eve please ladies?" Josh's persuading appearance ushered them out of the room. He looked frozen from his feelings as he stepped in.

"You know we are leaving child and you know I will be thinking and praying for us all to stay safe. I wish I could stay and watch your light grow, but I have to return to Ireland. If you need us…"

"I know, it's ok. If it gets that bad I won't hesitate. I am a little scared of what's to come I must admit but I am strong. I know you will think of me everyday and I also will think of you, you woke me from my eternal sleep and I remember nothing but what is now."

Father Josh touched Eve's face and then opened up the case he carried with him; he placed the case on the bed. "Look, look at this glory, look at its power."

"The Sword of Justice, our Father's sword, the angel's sword of light." It gleamed on its sharpened surface, and it enriched Eve's soul with its power and its blessing.

"Take it." Josh lifted it with both hands from the case and placed it in Eve's, a great overwhelming feeling burst into her mind and body. She felt and saw a great bloody war between good and evil, the screams and struggle drummed in her head until she pulled herself back into the present.

"I saw angels, I saw the first war!" Eve stared into Father Josh's eyes as he took the sword from her and placed it back into the metal case.

"I will leave it here with you; it belongs in your care and hands."

"It was there the day I awoke wasn't it? The man that tried to kill me held it."

"Yes, it's the only way to kill an immortal soul. The sword will become part of you. Your power will defeat their followers on earth, but the sword will only be your true defence against the old watchers and any armies of fallen angels they have."

"Jin-Joel will know more of the rules on earth that I have to play with won't he?" Eve suggested a little anxious. She still had much to learn.

"Jin-Joel is wise and can teach you many great things, but you will also have to study the scripts too." Father Josh closed the lid of the case and walked out of the bedroom, Eve followed him to the lounge area forever thinking about her new teachings and what they would bring.

As the sun began to set Eve wandered into the temple and found a foot rail out the back door that ran on to the roof. She climbed the foot rail to the top and stared into the sky and watched the red flames sink lower and lower into the city. Her head now cleared and thoughts of the day drifted off in her mind. She hid any emotions from everyone as Josh and the others left to go back to Boyle, she didn't want them to think her heart wasn't strong enough to cope without Father Josh.

It was a nice climb up to the roof, and the view of some of the city was enough to know somewhere out there people were getting on with life blissfully unaware of the truth; of where life began and what was hidden out there in the darkness, and waiting in the shadows. Eve knew only too well and she felt the darkness, yet she was here to light the way.

The ticking of the clock grew louder as Eve heard the new day and it made her spring up from her sleep. "It wasn't a dream" she explained to herself, "I'm still here!"

Eve had five minutes to go before the alarm would sound. "Oh, five forty-five in the morning." She threw back her covers and made her way to the bathroom. The cold water on her face made her take a sharp breath before she splashed more all over her face and neck. She threw on some clothes and made her way up the tinny sounding steps. The door to the gym was already open when she reached it.

"Jin-Joel... What time do you rise in the morning? I feel like I have been running all night."

Jin-Joel turned to face her from his Thai Chi and smiled. "Hi Eve, welcome, hope you slept well, ha, you will get used to the early mornings. Oh and I wake up at four thirty every day."

"Four thirty! Wow, you must be mad. No I'm just joking. I can see you are very dedicated."

"And you are also, I can see in your heart; your strength."

Jin-Joel showed Eve some self-defence moves to throw an attacker straight on his back. They also practised on good timing when using attack moves. The use of special skills would become natural in her own way, but she needed to learn more defence moves, especially when it would be necessary to use the Sword of Justice.

Before she knew it time had passed and the clock read eight. "This has been great I feel so much more confident. Thank you Jin-Joel."

"You are a great student, now you must go and do some reading Eve; you have a lot to do!" Jin-Joel moved his hand towards the door as he spoke.

"Ok I will see you tonight at dinner hey?" Eve ran towards the door; outside teenage students arrived for their morning class with Jin-Joel.

"See you later." Jin-Joel shouted over the noise and hustle.

After a refreshing shower Eve strolled to the study; she opened the book left out for her, it was entitled 'Fallen Angels'. The chapters were taken from the scripts of Enoch, one of the first messages from the Lord of Light. Jehovah. It explains the account of the old watchers of the heavens who were meant to watch over us, to help and report back to the Skies. The script tells us how the first of the watchers; angels of heaven started to lust after the daughters of men. Lead by the angel named Samyaza who convinced two hundred other angels to accompany him on his mission of pleasure; because he feared to descend alone onto the earth.

Enoch explains how Samyaza had the desire to beget children by these women so they could have their own offspring and teach them the secrets of the heavens. The angels took oaths and bound themselves to Samyaza's mission by the undertaking of mutual curses, the pact was then sealed, and the betrayal was punishable with unnamed horrors.

The angels took wives and taught them sorcery; incantations and divination-twisted versions of the secrets of Heavens. The children of the angels became evil giants who ate and killed all they could.

The angels also taught men how to make swords, fabrication of mirrors and jewels. They taught how to use paints for dyes and beauty, so that the world became altered. Impiety increased, fornication multiplied and they transgressed and corrupted all the ways of the world. Men being destroyed cried out and their voices reached up to Heaven.

The Archangels Michael, Gabriel, Raphael, Suryal and Uriel looked down from heaven and saw the wanton bloodshed; they said to each other, "Earth deprived of her children has cried out to the gate of heaven. Souls of men ask for justice. King, Lord of Lords, God of Gods, thou who made all things, thou who possesses power over all, all things are open and manifest before thee. Nothing can be concealed from thee. The souls of the dead cry out."

The old watchers who descended to earth were written in the scripts, Samyaza, Urakabarameel, Akibeel, Tamiel, Ramuel, Danel, Azkeel, Saraknyal, Asaelm Armers, Batraal, Anane, Zavebe, Samsaveel, Erteal, Turel, Yomyael and Arazyel.

The Great Lord heard the cries and spoke, he sent Arsayalalyur, son of Lamech saying to him, "In my name conceal thyself and explain the consummation, earth shall perish, waters of deluge shall cover the earth and all will be destroyed." The Great Lord told Arsayalalur to teach the chosen few how to escape and how his seed may remain.

The Lord said "Raphael, bind Azazyel hand and foot; cast him to darkness, open the desert in Dudeel cast him there. He shall remain forever. Judgement to fire. Restore the earth which the angels corrupted, announce life so it may be revived."

"Gabriel, go to the children of fornication and destroy them all, let them perish by mutual slaughter."

"Michael, announce to the slain angels; the sons of impurity and bind them for seventy generations under the earth, burn them in the fires of judgement so it will last forever."

He spoke to the archangels, "Destroy all the souls addicted to dalliance, the offspring of the watchers for they have tyrannised over mankind. Plant seeds of life again cleansed from corruption, I will send blessings from heaven to descend on earth upon all labour of man. Peace and equity."

The angels, the watchers on earth called to Enoch the scribe to write a script of repentance and give it to the Great Lord. The Lord read his plead and told Enoch to explain his fury. Enoch told the watchers, "The Lord said that on earth they shall never obtain peace and remission of sin, they shall not rejoice offspring but behold slaughter. They shall never obtain mercy or peace. Be bound and never be able to return to the sky again." The watchers became terrified.

This was some of the scripts Enoch wrote from the word of our Lord; these were with the Dead Sea scrolls when they were first ever written before God's son himself was put on earth, even to this day it is said Jesus himself taught from these scriptures. The angels who watch over mankind now are Uriel, Raphael, Raguel, Michael, Sarakiel and Gabriel.

Eve looked up from the pages; it began to dawn on her just how long these dark demons had been plaguing the earth, taking in more souls each day, jumping from one generation to the next and consuming all that was good and pure. It's hard to believe some religions don't even acknowledge these accounts at all, but just like the scriptures tell about the future to come just before judgement day. They tell about the wars in the east of the world, then the destruction of the earth from the natural elements. It tells us the days will become nights and the weather will begin to change from winter to summer, the cold days will burn bright and the sun will freeze. This has already started! The terror has already begun to unfold; Eve's walk on the earth means judgement is here and now, and there is nowhere to run – nowhere to hide.

As Eve tried to rest that night strange thoughts and images passed through her head, an image of dark presence's played on her mind. She tried to focus in the darkness at the streetlight that drifted through the window in her bedroom, but still deep thoughts swelled around her head. The images of war and judgement were taking over her nights' peace; the pages of the book she had read from earlier tormented her. She rose from her bed and tried to fix her stare on the illuminated clock beside the bed, it read two thirty-five a.m. Eve walked from her room to the kitchen and as she pushed her hand to the wall to find the light switch a warm feeling flushed through her head, her eyes burnt slightly so she closed them and held her hand to her eyes. As she opened her eyes she realised something had physically altered in her body again. For now she could see in the darkness, she could see all as the light from outside reflected around everything and it brought a chilling feeling through her body.

Eve clutched a glass in her left hand and poured some cold water from the jug in the fridge, it tasted so refreshing and took away the anxiety she felt. Darrel stirred from his rest, she heard his groan as he probably realised the time. Eve saw a staggering figure walk from his doorway rubbing his head as he searched for the light switch by his bedroom door. Eve closed her eyes as she heard the zap of electric.

"Don't worry I will put the dimmer on. Have you any idea what time it is?!" He expressed that question with a feeling of torment.

"Yes I do know what time it is, just couldn't sleep. And be quiet Astra is trying to sleep!" Eve said with a concerned voice.

"Sleep, sleep does anyone sleep round here?" Darrel questioned.

"Darrel stop being a grump and go back to bed."

"Eve, are you ok? And why *are* you standing around in the dark?" A concerning look grew across his face as he walked on towards her.

"I'm fine, just the thoughts of the day running through my head. I didn't want to wake you both so I chilled with no lights."

As they talked it occurred to Eve that it wasn't just the pages she had related to today; she felt something more was about to happen and deep inside herself she could feel a strange energy which she could not place.

As Eve lay back down to rest she felt more relaxed. Talking with Darrel had made more reality with herself and her brain at last felt tired and hungry for sleep.

With her eyes closed she had empty thoughts and left herself open to the energy she could not place earlier, she drifted into the weary darkness. A face grew in the misty reaches of her dreams; Eve heard a voice calling to her growing closer. A figure in the mist stood in front of her, but she could not see the face. She tried to sweep away the misty shadows but it was no good. A feeling of uncertainty aroused in her mind; she knew who this was calling her.

"Eve, oh beautiful Eve. We need a little talk; I can only call to you in sleep, warrior."

"What do you want Lucas?"

"I just want a little chat, that's all and to show you that's all I want. We can meet in 'Deaths Grounds' so we can not use power!"

"Why do you call me in sleep?" Eve couldn't understand and that bothered her, but that is what Lucas wanted so she cut off the question with another. "Where do you want to meet?"

"St John's Grounds. The place is full of old sleeping rotten corpses; we can use no powers inside 'Death's Grounds'. Just remember we cannot enter the church, as they are unholy. This place is where we could fight 'til death; it is unsafe for me and of course yourself!" His ground groping voice stilled the echoes in her head.

For what he said was true, the temples built for the Gods were all unholy and were filled with unrequited love. Some of the first words of the Lord of Light had spoken was to love me in a place you would want to be alone to meditate your love. He had said build no temples in my name and no symbol in my image for I am the Lord of Light and my love is all around you. Churches were built at first to share their love, and then greed set in and it was all about possessing more. The old watchers spread their dark ploys from generation to generation and now they have taken over the love you believe in, which will save you. On Death's Ground is different, because there lay empty shells; forgiven souls sleeping. Some will walk eternally on earth until judgement, while others will obtain new skins and flesh after years of sleep; they will walk once again if good defeats the evil that plagues us. For no one will walk through heavens door until the day of reckoning. The offspring of the watchers are bound to the earth plains; even in death they cannot return to the skies but drift or be reborn as someone or something else. Sacred ground is where death is for no one has the power to destroy what is already dead.

Lucas's voice droned off into the distance with instructions that he wanted Eve to follow. Though she wanted to ignore this dream she knew he had made first contact and she was curious.

DEATH'S GROUND

Eve sat up in bed and adjusted herself to the darkness, the sun had begun to glow through the dark cloud, morning was here and she felt she had to leave now. The clock read four forty-five; Eve scrambled some clothes together and tied her hair back. She wanted to know if Lucas was really waiting for her or was it all an elaborate dream. Deep within, she knew...

Eve didn't want to disturb the others again but she couldn't creep through the window as it was placed halfway under the paved street. The sun was already sweeping across the streets outside. She crept from her room and made her way up the staircase. As she passed on through the bookcase she realised Jin-Joel was already awake. The light was on in the gym and the curtains had all been brushed aside to reveal the outside world.

As she walked past the double gym door a voice called out to her.

"Eve? Training early today?" She looked as Jin-Joel was walking up behind her on the bamboo matting in the hallway.

"Hi Jin-Joel, I would love to say yes, but something else is calling me."

"Lucas? It's a bit early to be looking for adventure; you still have much to learn!" Jin-Joel had already guessed, he could read her like a book.

"I just wanted to be sure, what if I was dreaming? What if I wasn't!? He said he wanted to talk on Death's Ground at St. John's."

"It is curious but I am advising you it may not be the right time for you. You have lots to learn, physical, mental and your inner being. I can't stop you from going, but I won't let you go alone." His eyes fixed on hers.

"I feel I have to go Jin-Joel. Sorry"

"Then I will be just behind you, I'll be watching." Jin-Joel assured both himself and Eve. For that reason Eve felt more at ease knowing that he would be there not for protection, but to make sure curiosity was all it was.

A black Honda Civic roared up under the trees outside St. John's grounds. Eve studied the area closely; she couldn't see anyone around at all which left a suspicious feeling in the air. Her senses had picked up nothing so far at all, but this was all still relatively new to her.

Eve shut the door and smiled at Jin-Joel as he reversed the car and drove further on past the rest of the grounds. The church stood right in front of her with six steps running up to the heavy old wooden doors. To the right were the old burial grounds, big heavy black railings ran all around the grounds. The new cemetery on the other hand was all open-planned with trees and plantation. The new grounds were not protected by outside forces, but inside them heavy black metal bars protected the grounds where angels could dare to cross and ponder sources together. Eve walked up the six steps in front of her; she was daring because she could consider this a wild goose chase because she couldn't sense any dangerous elements around her at all. She placed her hands on the dark wood in front of her; she paused for a second and then began to push the doors open. A powerful force pushed into her as she stepped inside, it felt like she was trying to catch the air to breathe. Her solar plexus burnt and she held her right hand to her chest. Suddenly she could breathe again, this place was unholy and she shouldn't be in a place filled with greed and power for control. As she walked a little more towards the altar she could feel a vibration getting closer and becoming more intense. The vibration was turning into a rumbling like thunder and it wasn't just under her feet anymore, it was all around her!

"Hello… Hello can I help you?" A priest stood in black watching Eve with concern; she appeared to have disturbed him from whatever he was doing. She didn't get time to talk to him as the ground started to shake, and the glass windows shook in their frames.

"What's happening? Who are you? What do you want?"

Eve tried to talk but couldn't even muster a squeak, she felt like she had no control of what was happening. Everything started to shake as the priest hid by the table at the altar; he held one hand in the air.

"WHAT DO YOU WANT!?" he shouted in a shaking voice.

"Judgement!" came from the air, from Eve's lips but she had no control of what she spoke, she couldn't break free from this hold – it was intoxicating.

The priest rose onto his feet and opened up the book he held, and started to preach and shout his words of God at her. The book burst into flames and he screamed in terror. Eve's body rose into the air and slowly twisted around as the stone figures crumbled around the church and the stained glass shattered. Glass filled the space around her and the candles sparked alight and lit the curtain drapes on the walls.

Screams and voices called out in Eve's head as the whole place was burning, she saw the terrorised look on the priests face as he watched her alight with flames all over her body. She screamed out as a ring of exploding light blew away her burning flesh.

Eve took a shocked breath of air and took her hands away from the wooden door; it was just a vision. She studied her hands and took another deep breath; she had never even entered the church but had seen what was to be...

Eve moved away from the doors, backing down from the steps, still concerned by what she had seen. In front of her the wind swept through the trees.

"I can feel you here." Eve announced with a raised voice.

Spinning herself around she saw a dark figure moving from the shadows from under a tree. Eves pulse started to race, she knew who had stepped before her.

"I only want to talk." The deep voice mocked her as he approached.

Eve could feel Jin-Joel near, and she also felt another presence.

"Lucas!" Eve said.

"Yes!" He answered as they both acknowledged each other. Lucas took the form of a dark handsome man this time; he was dressed in dark clothes with a long dark coat, maybe to hide the blade he was carrying.

Eve could not help but ponder the thought that Lucas is a pawn, acting on behalf of another.

"Why have you called me?" Eve asked.

"Why did you come?" Lucas replied, amused.

"I am curious of your plans." Eve answered.

"And I am of yours, but it is already written isn't it? Our mighty Lord of the heavens will wipe away all that is dark and cleanse the earth from evil. He will destroy what will not repent." Lucas mocked the beliefs of her followers.

"Who would have thought, God would have sent a woman, and let her name be Eve... Yes Eve the first to have fallen."

"I am not her! This kingdom you have built around you Lucas will all fall." Eve replied with great passion. She moved towards him to show him she wasn't scared.

"Eve... Why did you save Kate? In time she will turn against you all and you spoilt my plans for her. I will have her you know. I have so many followers; you have nothing, even the church worships symbols. The cross that killed our brother Jesus! What can you do?" He exclaimed.

"You're not fit to speak his name!" Eve replied.

"I will do as I am bid; the souls who can feel and care will repent to live and breathe our fathers love and those who choose not to will turn to dust. I will do this work with love not like your evil; you hide behind your own father. The beasts' power!" Eve enthralled.

"So do you!" Lucas replied sternly.

Lucas lifted his cloak and showed his blade, Eve had no defence with her, but herself. The blade glistened in the new day; it looked filled with rage and fire.

They were outside, not on Death's Ground so they could fight, was this what Lucas had planned all along?

Eve met with Lucas's eyes as she heard a voice holler to her.

"Eve, catch." Jin-Joel approached from the road throwing a covered sword towards her. Eve caught and drew the sword. "Thought you wanted to just talk?" Eve suggested, waving the sword towards the sky from her waist.

Before they even had time to make contact, two ghostly figures appeared from the smoky darkness.

The demons stood in front of Eve under the trees where Lucas stood. The demons waved their weapons at Eve as Lucas vanished back into the shadows.

"You are weak!" Eve shouted into the air, directed at Lucas.

Jin-Joel joined Eve's side.

"Careful Eve, these are just mere souls who have been taken over by Lucas's powers!"

"So what are you saying, I can't just slay them?" Eve asked anxiously.

"Try not to; we just need to extract the hold on them." Jin-Joel explained as an axe came crashing towards him.

Jin-Joel jumped out of the way and kicked the demon to the floor.

As Eve looked up one of the demons swung his sword at her, she jumped backwards as the blade tore her top, the second demon ran at her and jabbed her from the left. She jumped up into the air and flipped herself onto the steps. They both ran at her as Jin-Joel slid his body underneath them and they went crashing into the steps.

Eve jumped down from the steps standing over the two demons and spoke into them.

"Demon release them, powers of darkness leave these souls and go. RELEASE THEM!"

Dark smoke poured from the mouth and noses of the injured men as they lay unconscious before her. Now in their own form the two men looked young, Eve reckoned only in their early twenties. She felt a slight pain for them; they had been used because they had been weak in some way. She tried to brush her feelings away as she examined them, they were two drug addicts; the scars on their arms said it all.

Jin-Joel put his hand on Eves shoulder.

"What can you do? Eve we must leave before anyone arrives, I'm sure someone would have called the police."

"You're right, but I have to do something before we leave."

Eve held the first mans hand in hers and placed her other on his chest. She closed her eyes and imagined draining darkness from him and covering him with bright white light. The man's eyes, ears and scars all bled with the heroin that had once taken over him.

A white light then swirled through his chest on his solar plexus and he huffed a sigh of relief. Eve repeated this on the second man and the same white light burned within him, protecting him, healing him.

Eve stood up and held her hand in the air; she unclenched her fists as she released a dark dust into the sky, which burned up in the new days' sun.

Jin-Joel stood in amazement, "I knew this would be an honour and an unbelievable way of life to believe in, but this is truly amazing and so precious. You are Eve, daughter of the mighty Lord of Light." Jin-Joel bowed to her.

"Jin, I'm ready to leave. I feel pretty weak, I shouldn't have come."

Jin-Joel went and got the car. As they drove back home they both meditated on that moment.

BOYLE TOWN

Eve and the Sword of Justice

The breeze hit the trees and birds flew into the sky; Kate stood looking out from the window.

"I can help you and I can forgive you, but to trust you is the hardest."

Kate turned around, "Father I know I have let you down, but please... I would never do anything to hurt Eve, you know that." Kate said sorrowfully.

"Kate we all love you, I know you were not in your right mind, but what if you get confused again, then what?!"Father Josh asked harshly.

"It won't happen, I swear to God almighty." Kate looked intensely at Father Josh, "It will not happen again."

"I want you to spend some time meditating with the Elders; you need to spend some time to think alone without confrontation." He meant it in the nicest way, but Father Josh really meant away from himself and Martin.

Martin was on the phone to Darrel in his room.

"I'm ok Darrel, if I need some time away I will come and join you and Astra for a while, but I need time to think and look after Kate."

Martin caught a glimpse of Kate, "Got to go Darrel, Thanks."

"Kate, hold on a sec..." Martin leapt up to grab her. As she turned towards him her hair swung in all directions.

"I can't talk now Martin, I have to spend some time with the Elders and I have to get changed into my ceremonial clothes first." Kate sounded concerned.

"I love you Kate, I just want you to be safe and with me." Martin smiled at her with love; she felt more relaxed and assured as she cuddled him.

"I will talk to you when I can Martin, but I have to go now... I love you." Kate smiled back at Martin as she left.

Vern entered Father Josh's office with a cup of tea just as Josh switched on the TV. There were two young males on the news following an attack in London.

"We don't remember much, I just remember not feeling too well, when a man grabbed me and pushed me to the floor. Apart from a really pretty woman holding me, oh and I felt an energy I've never felt before, then I saw a white light, then I woke up in hospital." The young man was in his early twenties and was full of enthusiasm.

Father Josh looked at Vern with pondering eyes as the reporter spoke.

"This young man was found outside St. John's Church, he is a known drug user, a few people witnessed a struggle outside the church and an unknown woman covered in bright light. This man believes an angel was sent to save himself and his friend. We asked his doctor what happened to him after being brought into hospital."

The reporter turned to a lady dressed in a smart blue suit.

"Danny has been a known heroin addict for some time, after he was brought in with injuries this morning we checked his blood levels, only to find our results say there were no traces of drugs in his system at all. We thought that the tests were wrong and immediately carried out further tests only to be given the same results as before. The same happened to his friend as well. His injuries also seemed to have disappeared within an hour of him being admitted. I've never witnessed anything quite like it!"

The reporter turned towards the camera again.

"So were the two men saved by an angel or were they and the witnesses all suffering from an extreme case of overactive imagination? All I can say is the evidence suggests something quite unbelievable. This is Lisa Bailey reporting from London."

Josh flicked off the TV again and looked at Vern.

"Eve?" They both said together.

Josh picked up the phone.

Boyle Town was quiet mostly, but very busy in the summer months with the attractions of the monastery nearby.

Father Josh and Vern helped run the village unit where they lived, there were fifty families and they all ate together as well and all shared duties with cleaning this great big establishment and farming the fields for food.

The building they lived in was centuries old, it was made from large stones and flint. It had also been added to over the years. It was located a few hundred yards into a field with a dirt track running off into the forest and to the village road. The building had a stone wall to separate it from the village. It held twenty families in the walls of the building itself.

Martin and Kate of course lived there; Martin had joined in his early teens. He could be a bit of a tearaway and his mother and father couldn't cope. He soon became attached to this way of life though.

Kate was homeless, she ran away from a foster family at a young age, and she never knew her real parents.

Kate stood in the field at the back of the mansions grounds.

"STORM!" She shouted as snorts of an animal called back.

"Storm, here boy." The chestnut brown horse trotted up towards her.

"Hey boy, missed you, let's go for a ride."

Kate had attached herself to Storm while trying to forget her heartache in some recent events in her life. Kate loved to ride, she felt free and it released her from who she was.

Martin looked on from outside the back of the house.

"Hey Martin."

"Hi Shawn."

Shawn was Martins best friend and they searched out information together on local psychics and spiritual churches for later use. Shawn was fair headed and came from Scotland, his family had moved into the village about five years ago.

"Is all ok with you and Kate?"

"Not quite sure, found out a few things on our journey."

Shawn looked unsure for Martin and touched his shoulder; he quickly tried to think of something else.

"Martin, is it true about Eve, did she fight?"

"Yes, yes it was awesome." Martin smirked.

Martin explained to Shawn what had happened that morning and Shawn reassured Martin that Kate probably just needed time to herself.

Vern called out in the field to Kate.

"Kate you in the barn?"

"YES! Will be there in a minute, just putting Storm away." Kate soon appeared rubbing her head until her hair fell loose again.

"Martin was looking for you my love."

Vern placed Kate's arm through hers as they both chuckled.

"Oh it felt good, I feel so much better for taking Storm out." Kate grinned from ear to ear.

Martin lay on his bed reading as a pair of hands touched his feet then up to his knees.

"Hey!" Martin jerked as he looked from his book.

"Kate." He said smiling. She kissed his lips and touched has face. Then they lay together kissing.

Josh put the phone down as Vern entered the room, he had been talking with Darrel

"Well he says Eve is fine, but I ordered he make her rest from the outside world until the time is needed."

Knock! Knock!
Martin jumped up startled, "Kate," he whispered. Someone is at the door.
"So what, I have had enough of hiding! Come in." Kate sounded rebellious.
Shawn entered, "Come on guys get some clothes on. You both missed out on the talk."
"Look at the time Martin." Kate looked at the clock hanging on the wall next to the bed. It was 6p.m.
"You need to get dressed quick, communion dinner is ready." Shawn sounded slightly concerned as he left the room.
"We missed the talk Kate, on tactics and sending information to the others!"
"Martin we can catch up, Shawn will tell us." Kate was being stubborn and pushy.
"What's got into you Kate, you used to be in your books and wanting to know what was happening." Martin was becoming alarmed and Kate could see it in his eyes.
"Martin I'm ok, I just want some time for me, and I've had enough of living for someone else. It's ok I'm still here just had a lot to think about." She touched his cheek reassuringly.

Everybody started to gather in the big hall, three long tables were sat at the back and three at the front. All sat twenty seats each, the dinner was all placed in the centre of the tables so everyone could help themselves.
Martin walked through the first of the three stone doorways, Kate walked behind him, but before she could enter a hand grabbed her arm.
"You didn't go to the Elders as I asked, and you never turned up to the talk today, this is valuable information Kate." Josh let go of her arm and looked slightly frustrated at her.
"I thought you wanted my help Kate, and now I understand you spent the afternoon with Martin instead of your other commitments. What you were doing I don't want to know, but this can't carry on!"
"Josh I just need some time." Kate sounded like she just wanted to run away from the questions.
"Kate I love you, but if you don't want to be here anymore, then just say, instead of letting Martin fall away with you."

Kate looked at Father Josh with annoyed eyes as he walked away to greet the gathering.

"He doesn't mean that love, he just wants you to open up with us, so you can move on." Vern touched Kate's shoulder.

"Then why doesn't he just say that?" Kate uttered under her breath.

TRUTH SOMETIMES LIES SLEEPING

Darrel placed the handset of the phone down.

"Well that was Josh, he wasn't completely happy, but he said the news was very appealing."

Darrel looked at Eve and Jin-Joel.

"I better go to see the students." Jin-Joel said amusingly.

"You telling me off Darrel?!" Eve mocked.

"Eve, Josh said you shouldn't have gone out so soon, but you do what you like, we are here when you need us – at least you took Jin-Joel with you." Darrel slumped back down onto the leather sofa, looking up at Eve standing over him.

"Hey girl!" Astra walked passed and slapped Eve's arse.

"Heard you had a hands-on fight and I missed it. The two men or boys looked ok though. Well that's a good start to gain believers, hey!"

Astra stood in the kitchen, licking on a spoon she had just taken from the yogurt pot she held.

"What next?" Astra asked.

"A shower for me!" Eve replied.

"Want me to join you?" Darrel asked as Astra gritted her teeth at him in disgust.

Eve walked to the bathroom as Astra sat next to Darrel looking at the laptop he was working on.

"Josh is worried about Kate." Darrel said with concern in his voice.

"Why!?" Astra said digging into her yoghurt.

"Well, he said she is becoming very distracted from her work."

"I'm not surprised poor kid! What does he expect? Don't know why he doesn't send her to stay with us for a while." Astra suggested.

"Maybe he will…" Darrel remarked.

Eve stepped out from the shower and wiped her hand across the steamed up mirror. She looked at her face and then saw a reflection of someone behind her. She quickly turned around to find nothing there and when she looked back into the mirror the image was gone.

Eve remembered what Jin-Joel had said. He told her to practice making white light around herself, shutting her thoughts off from the outside, so nothing or no one could creep up on her without her suspecting first.

Eve drew her hands together and closed her eyes. She concentrated hard on the energy within the area around her solar plexus as a magical white light spun all around her and filled the room. It felt like a pair of wings being wrapped around her, it made her feel warm inside and protected.

"There's a Tarot and Psychic night in town, do you fancy it?" Darrel suggested to Astra.

"Why not, show Eve off a little if she wants, yes?!?" Astra smiled fluttering her eyelashes.

"See what she says, can't be as bad as meeting up with Lucas." Darrel said looking up from his laptop.

Jin-Joel's students were just leaving the gym when Eve stepped in.

"Master Jin, there is a Tarot and Psychic night in town tonight, I'm going along, what do you think?"

Jin-Joel stopped putting away the equipment and turned towards her with raised eyebrows.

"Do you feel ready? It will be very draining on your emotions. Make use of the white light around you, it will stop all the thoughts and emotions being overbearing."

"Ok Jin, but are you not coming?!" Eve looked at him for an answer.

"Not tonight Eve. You need to be around the others too, so they can get used to your powers."

Eve and Jin-Joel locked eyes and smiled at each other.

"See you later Jin, I'm going to study."

"Fancy hitting the shops Eve after your study hour? I'm getting my hair done." Astra explained excitedly.

"Ok, sounds good, I need to get some clothes for this evening."

Darrel held out his hand over the back of the leather sofa; he had about £400 pounds in his hand.

"Don't spend it all at once ladies."

"We will!!!" Astra said as she grabbed the money and ran up the stairs to join Eve, they could study together.

Outside it was hot and steam rose up from the road where the water had leaked from the flower stall.

"Hi Yvonne." Astra waved her arm at the lady rearranging the flowers.

"Hello Astra, out into the city?" Yvonne smiled.

"Yes, getting our hair done." Astra grinned holding on to a strand of her hair.

"Well have a lovely day both of you." Yvonne waved good-bye.

"You too honey." Astra giggled.

Astra held onto Eve's arm as they walked down the street.

In the city it was busy; the crowds were a little pushy.
Eve swallowed in the city air; hearing people's thoughts was becoming a little too intense. She closed her eyes and shut out what she heard. It wasn't long before they arrived at the salon.
"Hi, this is my friend Eve." Astra introduced Eve to her hairdresser Stu.
"Hello, you're new!" Stu said with a friendly handshake.
"Come and sit down both of you."
Eve looked at Astra and realised she had booked her in too.
"Hey, I knew you were up to something." Eve smiled at Astra.
"You don't mind do you? Astra asked.
"No, not at all, you're right I needed some pampering." Eve laughed.

Darrel was drinking his coffee in the kitchen; he had just been working out in the gym, when the girls arrived home.
Darrel nearly spat his coffee across the floor when he saw the pair!
"Wooo, you *have* been busy!" he said grinning from ear to ear.
Astra had her usual red and black streaks in her blonde hair, she loved to be wacky. Eve had blonde, black and purple streaks in her golden brown wave of hair. She had red leather trousers on and a tight long black t-shirt, which had the words "Rock Chic" in gold writing.
The girls had handfuls of bags and looked powerful and sexy already for their evening of adventure.
"We are trying to fit in." Astra smirked.
"You'll definitely do that!" Darrel said amused rubbing his chin.
"Well we are trying to relate with the people that will be around tonight."
Eve looked at Darrel's amused grin.

That evening Eve, Darrel and Astra arrived outside Eaton Hall – 1 mile from the City centre. Astra shut her laptop and looked up from the back seat of the cruiser.
Eve looked out of the front window staring into space as Darrel turned off the engine.
"Well, let's go!" Said Darrel enthusiastically.
"Are you ok?" Astra asked.
Eve looked up at Astra's reflection in the rear view mirror.
"I'm fine, just getting myself prepared." Eve smiled back at her.

Darrel slammed the cruiser door as they walked towards Eaton Hall. Eve stood at the steps before entering and listened as Astra and Darrel walked in through the doors.

Eve looked up at the building, painted all white with two old wooden doors; it looked like an old court house, now used for many different events.

There was music of a light mystic tone coming from inside the building as Eve felt a feeling of heartache, she turned to her right and saw a young girl on a bench.

Eve walked over to her, "You ok?"

The girl was (Eve guessed) about 15 years old, her eyes glistened in the light reflecting off the building from the street lights.

"Yes, I'm ok." She stuttered as she broke down into tears.

"You're not ok, what's happened, tell me." Eve used a caring down-tone voice.

"I just don't know what way to turn." She replied, obviously very confused.

"Didn't it help you in the hall?" Eve asked.

"Yes and no. It was nice to listen, but nothing has changed…" She stuttered emotionally again.

The girl wiped away the tears with the tissue she held.

"These places always tell you what you want to hear. You are in charge of your own destiny; God gave humans freedom of choice. What you choose to do will change your life and the events that follow. Evil has the biggest laugh knowing you find the answers in these false spiritual workings and not in your own heart." Eve looked into the girl as she stopped crying and looked puzzled.

"Who are you?" The young girl asked.

"My name is Eve, who are you?" Eve smiled.

"Jennifer. Eve is a great name." Jennifer looked at her hands and began sinking into herself again.

"Give me your hands, and let me help you." Eve opened up her hands.

"It's ok, I won't hurt you." Eve reassured her. Jennifer slowly placed her hands in Eve's.

BANG! A sudden scene of two people fighting stood in front of Eve. It was Jennifer's mother and father. They were shouting and pushing each other, Jennifer was up in her room packing a bag. She had enough. 'Slap'. Her father had hit her mother as Jennifer raced out of the door. She had been living on the streets now for a few months desperately trying to forget the pain, a pain that gnawed away at her inside.

Jennifer saw a light all around her, her head spun until it reached a vision of her family. She saw her mother and father crying together, they wanted her home. Her father was telling her mother "If only I could tell Jen I'm sorry and that we are getting help with our marriage." "It's ok love, she knows we love her." Jen's mother kissed her fathers head as they cuddled up together.

Eve let go of Jennifer's hands and they looked at each other in silence for a brief moment.

"How did you do that?!" Jennifer asked.

"You need to go home Jennifer." Eve said raising her eyebrows.

Jennifer smiled, got up and kissed Eve on the cheek and ran towards the station that was near by.

"Bye Eve, thank you!" She shouted as her voice trailed away into the distance.

Eve stood up, drew in a deep breath and walked towards the doors. The music hummed in her head as she entered the hall.

Eve nodded at Astra and Darrel as they looked around the tables that were selling jewellery and gemstones claiming they had healing properties.

"Was just coming to look for you!" Astra said.

"Wondered what you were doing." Darrel turned and stood pondering.

"I met a young girl outside who needed me." Eve wouldn't say more than that.

"I missed something else?!" Astra looked slightly disappointed.

Five tables in an 'L' shape in the hall were all dimly lit with candles – the hall was split in two with a thick black curtain. Behind the curtain a psychic was giving readings to people.

The tables were all assembled facing the centre of the hall and the tables selling 'mystic' items were facing the other tables from beside the wooden doors.

Eve started to walk around, looking and listening to all the conversations going on. It was not long before she grabbed the attention of the tarot readers.

"Like me to read your cards love?" A middle aged woman with white hair and glasses gestured at Eve.

"I don't think you can tell me anything I don't already know." Eve admitted. She looked at the flickering candles and crystal ball as she sat down in the chair opposite the middle aged woman.

"I'm Clara, what reading would you like?"

"I'm Eve, you choose the reading Clara." Eve said looking into the woman's eyes. Eve felt urges and struggles growing all around. Her being there was starting to have an effect on the atmosphere.

"You're not sure are you Love? Here you shuffle the cards." Clara handed them to Eve face down. Eve shuffled the cards and placed them face down in front of her. Clara smiled at Eve and took the first three cards from the pile.

"Death, Devil and the World, ohhh a new beginning for you dear, ohhh owww! The woman suddenly stood up with shock as all the cards in front of her started to smoulder from the middle and then burn on the table. The big wooden doors burst open as a gale of wind entered the hall, the crystal balls filled with smoke and the candles all blew out.

"What's happening?!" A man shouted from behind the curtain. "Argh!" A few screams were heard as people became concerned.

The doors slammed shut as Eve stood up; her eyes filled with a bright white light.

Astra and Darrel drew behind Eve as she turned to face the people who were starting to panic.

"It's you, it's your doing!" Shouted Clara pointing a finger at Eve.

A wild wind started to blow all around Eve, her hair blew around her face as the wind twisted faster and faster all around until she seemed just a blur. Suddenly bright lights spun around her and the twisting winds stopped. It was soon just a mild wind blowing through her hair.

"Eve what are you doing?" Darrel shouted through the panicked voices.

"Watch!" Eve demanded.

The bright lights flew and merged together in the air, everyone stopped talking. They looked up in stillness. Then suddenly the lights dropped down and bounced into and through everyone in the hall, and then all was still.

"I am Eve, I have been sent to you so you can find the truth. This place, these objects will not give you what you are looking for." As Eve spoke into the people the crystal balls shattered and tarot cards scattered into the air. Everyone looked like they were caught in time, suspended in animation.

"Psst, Eve". Astra tried to get Eves attention as Darrel elbowed her in the arm.

"Shhh…" Darrel snarled

"The one true thing is; Love... let that be your guide. Let the light show you the way. Live your life; fill it with magic, magic that you have all been given by God, the freedom of choice. You choose, let no one decide for you. These false spiritual workings are bad and will bring you closer to the darkness." Eve looked at them with a greatness assured that they would follow.

"Remember tonight and what I have said, all this searching for objects of desire is the wrong way. Now go and spread the word of what you found. The truth!"

The light grew more intense. As Eve spoke and the people listened, the light showed them visions of the fallen angels and their judgment, and the people were filled with feelings of fear and repent.

Eve still standing raised her arms into the air as the wind blew and spun around her once more. It summoned the light back into her being, until it was all still once more. The light faded from Eve's eyes as she turned towards Darrel and Astra.

"You both ok?" Eve asked.

"Absolutely awesome!" Astra excitedly admitted.

"Yer." Darrel smirked and felt on a high.

The people all gathered around Eve.

"Who are you?" A young man asked.

"I am Eve, angel of light and justice, here to bring forward believers and followers on the earth so you might repent your sins and live on again after Judgement Day."

Clara knelt down and kissed Eves hands.

"Please Clara, stand up..." Eve pulled Clara's hands up to make her stand.

"I am not your leader, but your protector." Eve announced.

"We should leave." Darrel insisted.

"What do we do now?!" A young woman asked.

"Go home." Astra replied as they walked away.

A crowd started to follow the three of them outside. As the crowd gathered they threw questions into the air. Eve turned to face them all as they reached the cruiser.

"Go home and remember what you have seen and heard tonight." She insisted.

All three jumped into the cruiser and pulled away from Eaton Hall car park. Astra was cackling to herself.

"I'm sorry, I just can't believe it, feels like we are in a movie." Astra giggled.

"Don't wet your knickers Astra, this is meant to be serious, did you see their faces tonight?" Darrel seemed stunned by the whole incident.

"Darrel!" Eve put her hand on his shoulder. Darrel glanced at Eve out of the corner of his eye, and tried to smile.

Eve felt a rush of energy as the car passed an open park on their journey home. She looked at the park on their right; looking past Darrel all she could see was the orange sky fading into the darkness against the trees around the square open field. To their left they past terraced houses with light dimly lighting the windows.

"Darrel, keep it steady and slow, we are not alone" Eve announced. She felt a dark energy creeping up on them again with that sinking feeling.

The wind rose up on the warm night breeze, and black clouds started to swarm in the sky above them. Astra sat up and looked through the glass in the roof.

"I don't like this!" She said as she felt a feeling of terror growing inside her.

"CRACK!" lightening hit out and sparked against the road in front of them. Darrel turned the wheel of the cruiser away from the strike as Eve shouted at him.

"STOP! Stop the car!"

There was a loud screech as the cruiser came to a halt. A tree fell in front of them with an almighty crash.

"Stay here." Eve insisted as she stepped out of the cruiser.

The clouds above shifted apart as a dark smoke drifted down to the ground.

"You should know by now Eve, every time you use your energy, I can feel it, and I can feel you."

Lucas emerged from the smoke, waving his right index finger at her.

"Playing games Lucas, your scare tactics don't fool me!" Eve faced downwards but looked up at Lucas in a frowning, threatening way.

"Playing games?! I only want to destroy you." Lucas taunted.

"Then destroy me, please try!" Eve moved her arms away from her sides to show she was not armed.

Lucas looked up into the clouds and called out…

"Shadows of fear and terror destroy her!"

Dark shadows slowly swarmed down towards Lucas as he held his hands extended towards the sky. Images and faces appeared in the shadows as they floated and descended. Four shadows remained as smoky silhouettes and images, two of them grew wings, horns and terrible beastly features; long black nails and razor sharp teeth.

"Eve!" Astra shouted desperately.

"Stay in the car!" Eve shouted over her shoulder.

"No way!" Darrel insisted.

"LUCAS!" Eve shouted into the night.

"Ha, ha, ha…" Evil laughter filled the night air.

The four shadow demons headed towards Eve as she looked around and stepped backwards. They moved around her faster and faster, trying to drown her with visions of pain and torment; a noise of panic – screams and cries. Eve closed her eyes, it was so intense, and she needed to shut off from these dark demons. She pictured her Lord of light and asked for his help. Eve imagined her body filling with light and energy and that it was bursting to get out. She opened her eyes again, they burned bright once more. The wind blew up again and spun all around her and the shadow demons. Then there was the light; that too spun around the demons. The shadow demons raced away from Eve towards Astra and Darrel who were outside the cruiser. Astra tried punching at the air to shoo them away.

The two beastly figures snarled into the air, their eyes glowing red and their teeth shown in full fury.

"Catch, Eve…" Darrel shouted as he threw her the silver case that contained the sword. Eve opened up the case; the sword glistened against the light of her eyes. Eve could hear her friends trying to fend off the swooping shadows, but her eyes were transfixed on the beasts in front of her.

Both beasts circled Eve; she closed her eyes and clenched the sword more tightly. As she looked up, one of the beasts swung at her from the right. She jumped out of the way as the second ran at her from the left. They collided together and stood dazed for a moment, then let off an almighty roar at Eve.

"Arrrrrrr, Grrrrrr!" The ground shook!

The beasts ran at her hoping to cause her pain as she spoke into the air.

"Strength of the air!"

The wind picked up in seconds all around, Eve's fingers tingled as she pushed her hands out in front of her. A blast of energy hit the beasts and they flew backwards into the road. Eve turned to Astra and Darrel, as they swung themselves backwards, forwards, left and right at the shadows.

"I've had enough." Astra protested.

Eve closed her eyes, pushed her hands in front of her and spoke, "Burning light, protect them."

The wind spun around Astra and Darrel as light poured from Eve's eyes. The light pulsed away from Eve into the wind swirling around her friends. Elf-like screeches filled the air as the shadow demons dispersed towards the sky.

Growling came from behind Eve; she took a deep breath and jumped into the air. She landed down hard on one of the beasts, drew her sword and lunged straight down into its skull, splitting it open. Moving quickly Eve kicked the other beast backwards towards the fallen tree and threw her sword, which sliced through the beasts' neck, killing it instantly. She withdrew her sword and stood back as they both slowly started to turn to ash.

More screeching came from the sky as the shadow demons descended once more. The three friends looked up as the demons grew closer. Eve brought the wind up once more; seven light beams spun around her getting faster until they became a blur.

The shadows now raced towards Eve along the ground and the light blasted away from her and into the eyes of the shadow demons. Screeches and screams grew louder and louder in the air as the light devoured them. They were no more...

Eve looked towards where Lucas once was, he had gone.

People emerged from lit doorways into the street to see what all the commotion was, or rather had been.

"It's all good, don't worry people. Just a fallen tree." Darrel hustled people away from the scene.

"I saw what you did." A little girl ran up to Eve as she hid the sword behind her back.

"What did I do?" She questioned softly.

"You killed them monsters." The little girl replied enthusiastically.

The little girl had been watching them from her bedroom window.

"Don't be silly Kitty! I'm sorry she has a wild imagination!" The girls' mother pulled her away from the scene, as Eve winked at her, suggesting she was right.

MENTALLY STABLE
PHYSICAL AWARENESS
BRINGS SOUND FOCUS

For two weeks all that was seen and heard in the news on the TV and on the radio were the events that had happened at Eaton Hall.

Eve was on the lips of the people, with talk of angels, judgement and myth, but Eve knew it was opening people's eyes to the truth with the stories and rumours.

Eve, Astra, Darrel and Jin-Joel trained in the gym during the day and studied with their books and the internet during the afternoon and evenings.

Father Josh rang at least once a day to give them any news they had for them in Boyle about any destructive forces starting from Samyaza and Lucas's followers.

Then in the last day of the two weeks spent focussing a phone call came from Father Josh, it was not the usual affair.

"Darrel I have a problem if you can help?"

"Go ahead Father, I'm listening…" Darrel said with concern in his voice.

"Kate and Martin are starting to spend too much time together; they are losing their focus on what needs to be done. Kate is starting to become very distant and destructive within herself… I thought it would be good for her to spend some time with Eve and the others for a while."

"Well when's she coming?" Darrel asked, trying to sound positive.

"Tomorrow Darrel, make sure it's ok with Eve and I will see you all tomorrow."

"See you tomorrow then, safe journey. Call me when you want picking up." Darrel said.

"Hey girls… We have a new guest staying with us; I'm picking her up tomorrow."

Astra and Eve looked up from the coffees they were both drinking in the kitchen area.

"Kate." They both said together.

"She can stay in my room; I will put out the camp bed. Hope she don't mind!" Astra glanced up at Eve.

"Sure it will be fine Astra." Eve smiled. Eve could feel uncertainties in the room. Kate obviously needed guidance still, but she was on a self destruct timer.

"Will just have to keep a close watch on her, won't we?" Eve looked at the other two – they knew in their thoughts what Eve meant.

"I will let Jin-Joel know what is going on." Astra sprinted off up the stairs.

"Do you fancy coming for an evening run?" Darrel asked Eve.

"Yer, sounds good. I will go put my jogging bottoms on!" Eve walked off into her bedroom.

It was 6:15pm and the air was still warm. There was a slight breeze, which felt delightful as Eve and Darrel jogged towards the back of the nearby shops and houses. The alleyways seemed like a maze, but they finally made it towards the river and a track that ran along the waters' edge.

Darrel and Eve ran for about 45minutes, until they decided to head off back home. They ran under a concrete bridge; they nearly got to the end of the bridge when three young men jumped out and strutted towards them.

They all looked in their late teens, dressed in ripped jeans and t-shirts. One stood in front of the other two, he held a knife.

Eve and Darrel stopped in their tracks catching their breath; they looked at each other as the men approached.

"Give me your watch!" The young man with the blade demanded.

"What?!" Laughed Darrel.

"I'm not joking!" He pointed his blade at Eve.

Eve stood in front of Darrel, turned and looked at him with expressive eyes. Darrel could tell she was going to take action.

The other two young men, one dark skinned, the other white moved closer to Darrel.

"Come on, don't be stupid." Darrel expressed as the man with the blade went to grab Eve.

Eve caught his arm and spun it around his back so he was facing the ground.

The other two men tried to grab Darrel. He elbowed the man on the left of him in the stomach and kicked the man on the right in the face. They both grabbed at their wounds and tried to make a run for it.

"Drop the knife!" Eve demanded.

He did what she said as she pushed him towards Darrel to hold as she ran after the other two.

"Sorry, so sorry..." The young man admitted, scared.

Eve ran up behind the other two men and kicked them in the back of the legs – they both fell.

"Where do you think you are going?!" She demanded.

They lay on the floor as Eve placed her hands on both of their heads.

"Get off..." They both shouted as they sunk in swirling light. They saw the outcome of their misadventures and felt strange fears of the people they had attacked in the past. They saw themselves in great pain, covered in wounds and blood as beasts and demons devoured them bit by bit.

"This is what it is like for the people you attack, you destroy them inside. If you carry on you will feel this great pain."

The men opened their eyes, they quivered and shook.

"Sorry, we are so sorry."

"Please, please!" They both cried out.

Eve walked away knowing they would recover soon and hoped they would seek a different way of life.

Darrel held the other man up.

"What you gonna do with me?" He asked in fear.

"Nothing, it's what you're going to do for yourself." Eve threw his knife in the water.

"Come on Darrel."

"What about him?" Darrel asked.

"He will find his own way alone now." Eve answered as the men ran away together.

The next morning Astra became fidgety when Darrel explained what had happened the night before.

"So can I tell Kate everything that's happened so far, or you gonna let her know how things go?" She asked Eve and Darrel.

"Astra, I think Josh would have prepared her before she gets here." Darrel said with a large grin.

"Bugger off Darrel, it's just exciting being a part of this isn't it?!" Astra's smile faded as she realised she was acting a bit over the top.

"Darrel. Time." Eve pointed to the clock.

"Yes, you're right, better be off. Be back soon." Darrel picked up the keys from the table in the living area and ran up the metal staircase.

A couple of hours past and then voices came from upstairs, Eve had just finished in the shower after practice in the gym, and Astra stood by the foot of the stairs.

Three people's feet emerged from the stairs as both girls waited to meet the two guests.

Darrel brought in two suitcases and placed them by Astra's bedroom door.

"Eve, hi how are you?" Kate sprung a cuddle on Eve, who felt her damp hair press against her neck from the clinch.

"Hello Kate, I'm great. You?" Eve said calmly, pulling Kate's arms away from her neck.

Kate seemed so childlike in Eve's presence, like she wanted Eve to take away all her fears and protect her. Kate nodded and rubbed Eves arm at the question.

"My dear Eve." Father Josh held out his hand and touched Eve's cheek.

"You have come so far in such a short time, you look good!" Father Josh smiled.

"I like your hair." Kate quickly punched the air with her words.

"Thanks Father, it's so good to see you, how long are you staying?" Eve grinned.

"Will be going back in the morning, wanted to see how you were all coping, thought I would have some time to talk with you all." Father Josh looked around at them one by one.

"Ok chick, sorry Kate, you're staying in my room, hope you don't mind? Shall we start to unpack?" Astra grabbed Kate's hand insistently.

The girls entered the middle bedroom door as Eve looked more dramatically at Josh, "What's going on Father?" Eve asked, slightly impatient.

"When you held Kate's hands that morning when we were outside The Bridge Inn, did you see her past?" Father Josh asked inquisitively.

"Yes, you know I did." Eve said sternly.

"No, I mean her childhood. The things she wanted to learn from Lucas?" Father Josh looked at Eve with the intention that nobody else should know.

"Yes, yes I did, and yes I saw the truth. It is ok, I know." Eve calmed her voice.

"I need her here so she can readjust her life." Father Josh looked at Eve intensely, and then his gaze turned as Astra's bedroom door opened.

"We understand Father, its good inspiration here. Hey Kate you'll love it!" Darrel turned and looked at Kate as he spoke.

Father Josh and Eve looked away from each other and smiled at Kate; she wasn't stupid, she knew they had been talking about her, but pretended she hadn't noticed.

"Kate, we're going to a spiritualist church tonight, do you fancy it?" Astra asked.

"Yes, ok, what do I do?" Kate replied.

"Just stick with us and be yourself." Darrel said.

"Let Eve do what she does!"

"I don't think I shall attend this evening, I have made plans with Jin-Joel, we need to have a little chat on the latest events." Father Josh put down his leather case and sat on the sofa.

"Any chance of some coffee then?" He smiled at Astra.

"Yes, yes, I'm on it." She walked over to the kitchen and flicked down the switch on the kettle.

The evening came and Eve meditated in her room with the Sword of Justice, talking to the Lord of Light, telling him of the days' events and what they were going to do that night. She asked for his guidance and protection for the events that were to follow.

'KNOCK, KNOCK' Darrel pushed open Eve's door.

"You ready?" He asked.

"Yes." Eve opened her eyes and placed her sword on her belt in its sheath. She hid her blade under the long black leather coat she wore.

"Do we all have a weapon this time?" Eve asked. Kate looked very concerned.

"Nothing to worry about Kate, just have to be ready in case." Darrel smiled and placed one hand on her shoulder.

Astra produced a gun, as did Darrel.

"What the hell do you need them for?" Kate said anxiously, "Thought you were joking?!"

"They might not do much but stun something for a while, but that's all we need right?" Darrel asked Eve.

"Yes, that's about right. Eve said looking at Kate.

"It's ok!" Astra mocked.

"Come on!" Darrel insisted.

They had to drive to the west side of the city to Necton Spiritualist Church. They arrived at 8:30p.m.; the meeting had already begun. Darrel parked on the opposite side of the street. It was quite busy with cars parked everywhere outside.

"What's gonna happen in there Eve?" Kate asked.

"Nothing too bad. Just making them see the truth Kate. You can stay here and wait in the car if you like." Eve stopped walking towards the church and looked at Kate.

"No, no I want to see, I trust you." Kate told Eve, and herself.

All four of them made their way on towards Necton Spiritualist Church, Darrel pushed the black gate open and they made their way in through the small doorway. A man greeted them and told them where to sit. Everyone was singing from a spiritualist hymn book that they were given at the door.

The hall was the size of a football pitch; seats backed up to the wall on three sides like the stands, making sure everyone could see the centre wherever they sat. There were four columns on each side and three high rows of seats. The man pointed the four of them to the right, second row in the middle.

Everybody had just stopped singing when the four friends got themselves seated.

"Thank you everyone that was wonderful."

An old man of about 65 years clapped his hands together in the centre of the hall.

"Ok, we have a lovely guest here to help us talk to loved ones who have passed on. This is John Walters; please join me in giving him a warm welcome."

Everyone started to clap as a middle aged man of about 50 years made his way to the centre and waved to them all. He was dressed in a light brown suit with a shirt and tie. He had dyed dark brown hair and a golden complexion like he had just come back from his holidays.

"Hello, first I want to say thank you for a lovely greeting before I start looking around."

He smiled at everyone then started pacing around taking in the atmosphere. Everyone went very quiet and still.

"Hmm… Can anyone give me the name of Olive? She passed on about 5 years ago; she spent a lot of time in hospital." Nobody answered.

"Come on people." He walked over to a young couple at the front on the left side of the hall.

"Hmm… She says the lady in the yellow top knows me, I was a friend of her grandmother." The man looked at the young lady. "Has your grandmother passed away love?" He asked her.

"Yes a while ago, but I don't remember an Olive." The young lady answered confused.

"Well Olive just wanted for you to know that she watches over you for your grandmother and that the decision you made over that car was right." The young lady looked puzzled and shocked.

"Oh ok, well the new car is much better." She laughed.

"Ok, thank you love, if people call out when they know who I might be talking about it will help or I have to send the spirits away!" John circled the hall again and was quiet for about 3 minutes.

He looked very much in a trance. As he raised his head he stood still and then looked around the room.

"Christine! Does anyone know a Christine or Chrissy?"

"I do!" A man stood up in the 3rd level beside the four friends.

"Alive or passed on?" John asked.

"Alive." He said.

"No, sorry this one has passed on. Does anyone know an Eve? She has a son named Michael." John stood with his back to the friends. Kate looked at Eve.

All the hairs on Kate's neck stood on end and she took a deep breath.

"Eve…" Kate whispered.

"Don't!" Astra grabbed Kate's arm, but it was too late, and Kate managed to say one word into the air.

"I… ahhh…" Kate stammered as Astra pulled her back into her seat.

The lights began to flicker in the church and a breeze picked up from the floor.

"Move, move out of my way." Eve said to the others.

"OK, MOVE!" Darrel shouted to the others as the people around them started to show concern.

The wind caught hold of John as he spun himself around and stared at Eve, his eyes filled with blackness; he tilted his head to the side.

John was becoming consumed with Lucas's energy.

Eve closed her eyes and meditated on the white light that protected her, she opened her eyes, and they gleamed brightly.

"Demons behind closed doors show yourselves!"

It felt like a bomb had hit the air. Everybody gasped as the dimension that hid the demons was taken away. People turned to look at each other panicking at what they could see; images of smoky figures whispering in peoples ears. They were all round them sweeping around the room. People screamed and ran towards the exit as the demons mocked them and blocked the way.

"It's locked, we can't get out!" A man screamed as he banged on the door.

The breeze caught Eve and twisted all around her, followed by seven light beams. They all spun around her until she looked like a blur. Then the beams spun off and hit into everyone making them stand still, suspended in time.

"Eve, not again, we should stop meeting like this." Lucas talked through John Walters, standing there staring with his dark black eyes.

"Lucas you coward, let him go!" Eve demanded.

"A-haha... Don't make me laugh. Oh Eve how thoughtful, you brought me a gift. Hello, Kate." John grinned.

Kate cringed and moved towards Darrel.

Eve looked at Kate then back at John. She closed her eyes as the light and wind spun around her once more, the light beams soaked into her through her solar plexus. She stood up on top of her seat.

"These are what plague your emotions and give you signs, not your dead loved ones, but these demons. They come to you with pretence to make you turn away from the truth. They come into your heads at night, into your lives and mock you. They move objects and whisper paranoid messages of delusions... Your dead loved ones are sleeping, until they will be woken by God our father! Cast away your shadows of doubt and you will be free!" Eve spoke to all present.

'CLAP, CLAP, CLAP' John clapped his hands in amusement.

Kate wondered if Lucas really did know of Eve's past life or was it the smoky figures had picked up her passing thoughts.

"Get her!" John pointed at Eve and the smoky figures all assembled in the room together above him.

They all circled above John, and then they sprung out in all directions taunting Darrel, Astra and Kate. They circled them whispering their names and taunting them with visions of deep disturbing horrors.

"Kate, Katy, we know what you want." Kate put her hands on her head and crouched towards the floor.

"Arrrggghhh... Stop!" Astra demanded, holding her head.

"Eve." Darrel shouted.

The smoky figures showed them haunting images of torture and pain. Their voices were sounds of taunting pieces of lost memories. Eve raised her arms in the air and walked towards John and clenched her hands together.

"Air and light protect me." Eve threw her arm out, drawing air and light energy from all around her and from within; she punched the air towards John. John threw up his arms, he had no protection, Lucas talked through him, but had no real power within his body.

John flew backwards onto the floor. Eve stood over him and placed her hand on his head.

"Release him!" Eve gritted her teeth.

John's body shook and his eyes rolled. White light glowed in his solar plexus and his eyes then cleared. Eve let go of him; he lay still.

Eve turned to her friends, the smoky figures had disappeared. She looked down at John; he grabbed his head and sat up, as she stood over him.

"You are being used as a tool to speak words of lies to innocent grieving people." Eve moved her face near John's and looked at him scouring. She grabbed his shirt and pulled him to his feet.

"Hope you have learnt something." Eve said as she let him go. John stood with his mouth open.

"I didn't know, I didn't…" He tried to assure them.

"You do now." Darrel said as he helped Kate to her feet.

The other people began to move around again as Eve and the others left the church.

"What was that?" The friends heard a voice shout.

"Who was that woman?" Another person said as a crowd of people moved quickly out of the building.

The four friends jumped in the cruiser; Darrel started the engine.

"You ok Kate?" Eve asked.

"Yes, don't think I'll do it again though." Kate insisted.

What Kate said amused Darrel and he let out a sudden burst of laughter, "Ahahahah… Sorry, it's just I can understand how you feel, I felt like that when we went to the psychic fair two weeks ago, but after the little break it gave me time to adjust and think." Darrel tried to be understanding as they drove away.

"Eve, how do you feel with all that energy inside you?" Kate asked.

"Whole and pure, I feel strong inside. I want to protect everyone. It does give me a good head rush, but weirdly it feels natural too." Eve turned to Kate whilst talking. Kate lowered her eyes; she was filled with wonder and fear, but felt safe by her friends' side.

Astra was quiet, she was looking out of the car all around thinking to herself about the voices she had heard from the shadowy figures. They had sounded identical to people she knew that had died over the years, but she knew it was all mind games.

They were ready if Lucas wanted another showdown, but nothing disturbed them on the journey home, and that was disturbing enough to think about.

Early the following morning Astra woke Kate, "Hey girl you coming to the gym?" Astra shook Kate on her arm as she lay with her back to Astra. The camp bed squeaked as Kate sat up, "What's the time then?" Kate blinked her eyes.

"It's six a.m., come on it will be fun." Astra tried to make it sound exciting.

"Ok, ok, I'm up!" Kate tried to climb out of her bed, but fell backwards again, the girls both giggled loudly.

"Sounds like they're having fun." Darrel said to Eve as they walked up the stairs together.

Hi Jin-Joel, hi Father Josh." Darrel held a hand out in the air to say hi as he heard two other pairs of feet running up behind him and Eve. It was Astra and Kate, they were still giggling from Kate falling back in the camp bed.

Jin-Joel and Father Josh now stood with their arms behind their backs in front of the fighting ring at the back of the hall. The four friends now stood facing their teachers.

"Is everything ok?" Eve asked concerned.

"Yes, we were just discussing what the reports are saying on the TV again today." Father Josh said.

"Demons and Angels, the end is nigh, oooohh!" Jin-Joel was mocking a previous radio report from a witness at the scene last night.

"I will be leaving soon, so I want you to carry on and be careful... Glad to see that Kate is going to start to practice in the gym with you all." Father Josh beamed a smile at Kate; she did look a lot happier than she had been in days.

"Was it ok for you?" Father Josh walked towards Kate with a caring tone and approached with his arms open down by his sides.

For a moment Kate looked at Father Josh with a puzzled gaze, then said, "Yes it was fine. A bit more disturbing than I thought it would be, but it was fine. Eve protected us!"

"So you will be alright here if I leave now?" Father Josh looked into Kate's eyes trying to be reassuring.

"Yes it's fine, promise." Kate insisted.

A week past and one morning when they were finishing off with their exercise lesson Kate walked through the gym towards Eve, who was wiping her face with a blue towel.

"Kate, what's up?"

"Can we do something tonight, thought it would be good to have a break." Kate asked fearing the answer.

"What were you thinking?" Eve asked.

"Well I haven't been to a night club before! Wondered if we could go see what they're like." Kate was dreading what Eve might be thinking.

"I don't know if that's such a good idea, well not for me! Why don't you see if Astra is interested?"

Eve felt bad, but she knew when people intoxicate themselves with substances out of their depth it leaves them open (mind and body) to all sorts of unmentionable things. Eve couldn't be around intoxicated people, they would become better targets for Lucas. He would be able to completely corrupt their minds.

"Sorry." Eve said hoping she had not offended Kate.

"It's ok, I already asked Astra...She said she would rather itch her arse!" Kate seemed really disappointed.

"Kate, let's go and have a coffee, you're probably just bored and need to meet people, there is a rock bar a few streets down, we can go there if you like." Eve tried to make her feel better.

"Ok, think I will give Martin a call too." Kate turned away feeling slightly let down.

Astra stepped from her bedroom as Eve walked in.

"Astra, coming for a coffee, I'm just gonna get changed."

"Yer sure... Did Kate ask you about clubbing?" Astra asked.

"Yes, I said clubbing who" Eve mocked. "Yes she did, I told her it wasn't a good idea I went. Why are you not going?" Eve seemed a little confused.

"I fancy having a nice boogie on down, but what I don't fancy is some pissed up yob cracking on to me and falling all over us. Oh and I knew you probably wouldn't go." Astra looked at Eve trying to win her over to say yes, and then they all would go.

"No way Astra! I'm not leaving any intoxicated people more open to chance! Poor Kate, she looks so disappointed. Why don't you just go for an hour?" Eve knew Kate was starting to feel down again.

"Well I will see how I feel later." Astra said.

Darrel was out with Jin-Joel sorting out food supplies for the month, so they wouldn't be home for another couple of hours.

Kate was on the phone to Martin discussing how she was feeling.

"Kate, I'm sure it's for the best, you don't know the area too well. I'm sure Eve and Astra have their reasons." Martin tried to assured her.

"I know, it's just I'm bored and I've never been to a nightclub before!" Kate droned.

"Kate I have to go, I love you, stay safe ok? Miss you."

"Bye, I love you too." Kate gradually put down the receiver of the phone in the study and huffed disappointedly.

The bookcase suddenly slid back beside her and alerted her senses with a jump!

"Oh." Kate jumped back.

"Hi girly, morning coffee awaits." Astra announced.

Astra and Eve stepped into the room. Eve slid the bookcase shut, then all three walked on outside, through the double doors onto the street.

Three streets away, moving more into the city was the café, facing a paved square centre where a few shops met facing each other.

The café had smoked glass windows and outside were two round tables with three chairs around each one. There the three friends sat drinking their coffee. Rock music filled the air inside and outside the café, while customers wandered in and out, getting their morning fix ready for work.

The three girls sat talking about the events posted on the internet about the evening at the spiritualist church.

"I hated those voices around me." Kate said.

"Yer, they were very demonic – felt like they were taking me over at one point." Astra explained.

"The people that witnessed it all hopefully won't go to any events like that again." Kate explored the idea in her head.

"Well hopefully they examined that evening and realised they should pay more attention and time to better things." Eve sat up and thought how she would have felt being in the others' situation, it would have made her more aware of the good and bad forces working on this earth, playing with our emotions and minds.

Just then two young men sat down on the table beside the girls, the waitress came over with a girl, their body language suggested that they all knew one another.

"So you coming then Lou?" A pretty, skinny blonde girl stared at the waitress as she sipped her coffee.

"Suppose, what time you gonna be there?" The chubby waitress lent over the girls' table and placed the empty cups on her tray.

"Thanks." Eve smiled at her.

The waitress glanced at her friends for an answer.

"8p.m., we can meet you here if you like?" One of the young men suggested.

"Ok see you here then." The waitress walked back into the café jingling her tray as she left.

Just then one of the lads tapped Eve on the shoulder. "Have you got a light?" He asked holding a cigarette in his fingers.

"Don't be rude!" The young girl said penetrating his gaze.

"It's ok, and no I don't smoke." Eve said with a smile.

"You girls got fellas then?" He cheekily smiled.

"No, and well you're a bit young don't you think?!" Astra stirred her spoon into the last dregs of her drink.

"I'm nineteen actually, was just admiring three pretty women." He replied.

Astra laughed out loud and Kate giggled.

"Leave them alone Toby." The young girl prompted.

"Just getting to know them." He grinned at Kate, then went over and shook her hand, "Well, I'm Toby, this is Mark and Hannah."

"Hi."

"Hello." Everybody exchanged glances with each other.

"I'm Kate, this is Eve and Astra." Kate explained as they all shook hands.

"So what do you girls all do? You're models or something…" Toby asked.

"We are learning to teach martial arts and Astra is studying law." Eve replied.

"Hey, Kung Fu chicks!" Mark laughed.

"Charlie's Angels actually." Astra remarked.

They all giggled and chatted for a while. Toby and Mark were both studying art and language skills, while Hannah was hoping to start studying drama.

"You know we should meet up later, we are going for a drink tonight, then we might go onto a club." Toby suggested for the girls to join them.

"Not sure you youngsters might wear me out." Astra mocked.

"Well we are meeting here at 8p.m. tonight, would be great if you could come." Toby smiled again at Kate.

Eve stood up to leave, "We'll see, take care of yourselves, was nice to meet you."

"Might see you later then…" Mark winked at Astra.

"Yer… ha, ha, ha…" Astra laughed.

"Bye, was nice chatting." Hannah said.

The three friends walked on to look around a few shops before making their way home.

"What do you think Astra?" Kate asked when they sat down on the leather sofa at home.

Astra took off her shoes and stretched her feet.

"About what? The young people we met?" Astra asked.

"Yes, shall we go and meet up with them?" Kate asked excitedly.

"Not sure yet!" Astra said leaning her head back over the sofa.

"What's wrong with you lot, thought it would be more fun than this!" Kate said, as she jumped up and strutted towards Astra's bedroom, slamming the door behind her.

"She has issues." Astra looked at Eve.

"Maybe she does need to get out…" Astra stood up.

"I'll go and talk to her." Eve said, concerned.

Eve pushed open the bedroom door. Kate was sat on her camp bed staring at the wall.

"I'm being stupid and childish, I know." Kate said, still staring at the wall.

"Well no, I wasn't thinking that at all. I thought that maybe all the things that have happened to you have taken their toll on you and you just need to break free for a while." Eve sat down beside Kate, her face looked slightly stressed.

"It's alright Kate, you were shut away inside for a while and now you want to stand up and face the world with a vengeance. It's not the way I want you to feel. If you want to go out, there are better places I can take you." Eve said.

"I do… I did feel shut away. I don't want more than what I have now Eve, but for just a little while I want to know what it's like to be like them, the people we met today." Kate looked at Eve and then down at the floor.

"I will go with you Kate, but not tonight. I need to be slightly more stabilised. If I go with you it could risk some of the people there." Eve wished she could be more helpful, but that's all she could say.

A while later Darrel came in with Jin-Joel carrying four boxes of supplies.

"Hey up, some help would be nice!" Darrel asked as the boxes stopped him from seeing the last few metal steps.

Astra grabbed the top box and walked towards the kitchen.

Eve stepped out of Astra's bedroom and grabbed a box from Jin-Joel. They both smiled at each other.

"Hey Eve, there's a Pagan meeting tonight at nine, if you fancy it?" Darrel looked towards Eve and Astra.

"I'll do some research on Pagan meetings and worship in August and September." Astra said stretching up to the shelves in the kitchen to put some cans of food away.

"It's good with me." Eve said, she was still thinking about Kate, maybe this was a bit too much for her and she would be better off returning to Ireland. Before Eve had time to tell the others of her concerns, Kate emerged from Astra's room.

"Pagan meeting tonight Kate?" Darrel said as he nodded to Kate as a greeting.

"We going are we? Don't fancy bumping into Lucas!" Kate said raising her eyebrows with concern over the last time they met.

"Kate's right, it's very likely he will be near and she doesn't need that right now." Eve said abruptly.

"If you want to stay here, it's ok with us Kate." Astra looked at Kate's face, she looked pulled in two directions.

"I'm not too sure?" Kate sat on the sofa and watched the others.

"I would like to come with you." Jin-Joel said to them all, "You might need me." He felt a feeling of anxiousness that Lucas might be on a stronger form with the believers of the Magic Circle that worked as they thought, in harmony with nature. Really it is another working of something else.

Astra looked up from Darrel's laptop. "It's a lunar meeting tonight, the one before the Autumn Equinox on the 26th of September."

"Six Bells Barn, at Channel Farm, East from the city!" Darrel explained.

Jin-Joel looked at them all. "We all need to get prepared."

Later that day, Eve stood on the roof top staring over the city. A breeze caught her and blew her hair away from her face.

She wore all black; she was preparing her thoughts for the evening. Something was not quite right; Eve sensed a darkness of what was to come, but she could not place what it was and this concerned her.

"EVE!" Darrel shouted as he emerged from the fire-escape stairway on the front of the building.

"We have geared up the car, are you ready?"
Eve looked sideways towards Darrel. "I want Kate to stay here!" She
announced.
"Ok, I will let her know. Is anything wrong?" Darrel asked with a slight
concern.
"Just a feeling I have." Eve said as she walked towards the fire-escape
railings.

They all sat in the car, Eve sat next to Darrel in the front, she looked at
her watch.
"We need to be early," Eve turned to the others, "assess the situation,
there are usually at least thirty to forty people at these little meetings and
a couple of hundred sometimes at the bigger ones."
Astra remembered the studies she had done before Eve came to be.
"Should get there for 8p.m., an hour early, can see them start preparing."
"Good, good." Jin-Joel looked towards the front.
Everyone concentrated on the road ahead as they made their way through
the city.

Kate was sat on the sofa flicking through the channels on the TV.
"Boring, boring, rubbish, boring…"
Thoughts of going out and having fun soon came into her head, then
dispersed with thoughts of the others and what they would say if she
abandoned her concerns.
Kate breathed in a sigh, "That's it, I'm going to go, maybe just this once,
I want to see for myself." She told herself as her heart filled with
excitement.
She ran off to Astra's room and flung open the wardrobe doors. She
pulled out a sparkly denim skirt and a long tight silver wet-look top. She
found Astra's long black leather boots too. "These will do." She said
slightly nervous, unaware of the feelings creeping around inside her. She
had never dressed like this before, what would she look like? Never mind
that now, she needed to have a shower!

Kate wiped the steam from the mirror, dressed in a white towel. She
started drying her hair with the hair dryer. "What do I put on my face?"
she thought.
She poured out Astra's makeup into the sink and pronounced her face as
Astra did. Blusher, eyeliner, and dark red lips. She rushed to the bedroom

and checked the time, "7:30! Oh got to be there at 8!" She remembered the others from earlier. Mark, Toby and Hannah had said they would all meet at the café.

Kate zipped up the boots and stared into the mirror, she resembled a younger Astra on a night out. "Oh wow, my God, look at me. I look, I look, ok!" She was beaming and beautiful, not too over-dressed, definitely good for clubbing. Kate did worry slightly though, mainly because she had never dressed like this before, she felt a little shy.

Darrel, Jin-Joel, Astra and Eve approached the farm area; they parked on the track just inside the forest area, and away from prying eyes.

They emerged from the car, Astra hid a small blade by her ankle and Eve placed her sword in its holster on her left side.

They slowly approached an area where they could see people arriving in a nearby field at the farm.

'Seven Bells' looked quite small from the outside. It had an old looking white wooden front door, a small stone driveway to the right and a small front garden to the left with bushes that hid the left front window of the house away from the farm track that ran outside. The left downstairs front room light was on. Inside the curtains were all shut and the front porch light was on, glowing a soft amber colour.

It seemed so peaceful and quiet, with the fresh smell of grass filling the air mixed with a slight hint of wild rose.

The four friends hid themselves in amongst the bushes and shrubs just outside the field. They were at least a good 30 feet away from the gathering that had started to form. They looked away from any passing cars as the headlights caught the bushes where they hid. Darrel got two pairs of binoculars with night vision from his black rucksack.

"Have a look Eve." Astra said as she passed a pair over.

"When the rituals start, we can move in closer." Darrel said.

"Do you think we could gain followers from these people Eve?" Astra whispered.

"Depends on what they believe is good or evil. I might be demonic or possessed in their eyes, like with many religions," Eve whispered back, "You never can tell..."

Kate pulled her skirt down and sat down on a bench opposite the café, she checked her watch. It was nearly 8p.m., she glanced up.

"Kate isn't it?" Hannah had arrived with Mark.

"Hi. Yer. Is it ok if I still come with you?" She asked.

"Course it is," Hannah said, "You look great!" She sounded happy Kate had showed.

Mark grabbed the girls by the arm in a friendly gesture, "Toby's here."

Toby walked on towards them shuffling his feet.

"Lou can't make it," he explained.

"Ok will ring her later." Hannah said with slight concern.

"Hi, wow, Kate, right? WOW!"

"Well, what bar first?"

"Orleans." Both the boys shouted.

Hannah linked her arm with Kate's as they walked into the city.

Candles started to be placed in a circle around the field and then an altar was assembled with old chopped logs as a long cloaked figure sprinkled rose water over it muttering words into the air.

"It's a blonde woman," Darrel said, "Hubba, hubba!" He mocked.

More people gathered inside the candle lit circle, most wore dark clothes; others wore cloaked garments, everyone seemed happy to see each other. When everyone had made their way on in the circle, a fire was lit just outside the circle, with a small one lit in the altar in the centre of the circle.

It had started.

'Orleans' glowed the big blue sign; the floor was filled with loud talking and laughter. Kate wasn't used to intoxicated crowds and made her way to the bar with Hannah.

"Kate, what you drinking?"

"Erm… Coke, don't know?" Kate said unsteady as she looked all around her.

"Coke?" Hannah said surprised. "Hey mate two double Vodka and Cokes please." Hannah shouted to the man behind the bar.

"Here drink this it'll loosen you up a little." Hannah said passing her the drink.

Kate took a swig, "Phwor, what's in this?"

"Vodka, just drink it." Hannah said knocking hers back and producing another from the bar.

"Kate we are gonna have some fun ok." Hannah insisted.

"Ok then." Kate replied unsure.

The smell of burning wood filled the air as a woman approached the altar.
"Here we go." Whispered Darrel in the bushes.
The woman was dressed in a dark red gown. She stood on a log to gain
more height and placed a silver bowl in front of her.

Kate and the others had now consumed a few drinks and made their way
to Ricardo's night club, where people had began to queue outside.
"Shouldn't be waiting too long." Mark said as they joined the line outside.
"This is so good, think I'm a bit tipsy, can't wait to see what this place is
like." Kate said infused with excitement and alcohol.
"It's great to meet new people, but Kate if it does get too much for you
let us know and we can chill out." Hannah smiled at them all.
"Yer, wouldn't want to make a bad impression on your first meeting."
Toby grinned.
"I'm good, and don't worry about me. I am so glad to be out having fun."
Kate moved forward as the line started to disappear inside the banging,
beating doorway.

Eve and the others watched as the woman addressed herself and threw
her arms into the air.
"Welcome everyone, tonight is the beginning of the celebrations before
the Autumn Equinox, we are gathered here tonight to celebrate the
turning of the seasons with nature. Welcome!" The lady looked at all the
faces present.
"Welcome!" The gathered souls said together.
"We will do some simple rituals to contact our deeper consciousness and
widen our spiritual powers, so we can be at one with the changing faces
of the Gods of the Seasons."
The Lunar Moon could be seen in the sky as the night started to settle in.
Chanting voices were beginning to rise in the night air.
"When shall we move in?" Astra asked in a hushed voice.
"When they start to begin their rituals, they will meditate into a deep state
while leaving themselves open to outside forces. About then, hey Eve?"
Darrel suggested.
Eve could feel something else…Not where they were now, but
something else was stirring amongst her friends. She could feel it, but not
see it. What was it that she could sense?
"Sorry Darrel, yes while they converse their thoughts in meditation and
their pretend Gods." Eve spoke with general rule.

Kate danced with a great smile on her face as Hannah moved closer towards her, "Hey there's a handsome face in the crowd that keeps following you." She said in Kate's ear.
The music drummed hard and loud, pounding their heads like it was eating their minds.
"I'm already with someone." Kate shouted back. "Ok!" Hannah nodded.
A thin tall lad in a white t-shirt snuggled into the two girls as they danced. They both giggled as Hannah pushed him away.
"Was that him?" Kate asked.
"No, he's watching you over there." Hannah's finger pointed up to the railings behind them. As Kate turned around she could feel his staring eyes before she even saw him, but couldn't believe who she saw.
"LUCAS!" She gasped.

Flames flashed and grew higher as the woman threw substances into the fire.
She drew a sharp knife from under a blanket near by and sliced her middle finger, dripping the blood into the silver bowl before her.
"What you going to do when they reach meditation state Eve?" asked Jin-Joel.
"Fill them with images of me and of what has happened in the last month or two. Then I shall appear when they have opened their eyes from the disturbance and explain, I shall not be done until I have wiped the earth clean of Samyaza and his fallen angels' betrayal on their father and on the earth. Samyaza's son Lucas shall be the first to perish." Eve sounded haunted. Images were beginning to affect her, flashing images in her head of Lucas, blinding lights and distorted sounds.
Out in the field they had started the incantations and meditation, the others stood in the darkness, waiting to emerge and were getting ready for anything else wandering around in the darkness.
Stillness filled the air. Eve walked out of the camouflage and quietly walked towards them all, their faces looking towards the ground or sky with their eyes firmly shut deep in meditation. She walked towards the middle as the others looked on. She stood still and closed her eyes. Wind rippled up from around them all and swept across Eve, she breathed in and consumed the air they breathed. She concentrated hard and brought thoughts to her mind of all that was happening, all that was hidden from

the outside world. Eve placed her hands on the ground and opened her eyes.

She began to beam with white light, and the wind grew up around her, swaying her hair all around. She made sure her hands were firmly on the ground, onto the earth, "show them!" she instructed.

Beams of white and blue light, like lightening shot across the ground dispersing into each person open to outside forces.

Some people jumped a little, some opened their eyes too, but it was too late, they were all plugged into Eve. She would now show them what was really happening in the balance outside the walls of this dimension.

Kate turned and looked at Hannah with a panicked look on her face.

"Do you know him?" Hannah said sounding a bit confused.

"I have to go… now." Kate rushed her words, patted Hannah's shoulder and pushed her way through the crowds of dancers who were blissfully unaware. She couldn't see him anymore as she looked around desperately, but she also couldn't tell where she was heading… panic was beginning to set in. She saw the toilet sign for the ladies and made her way passed the corner of the bar to the doorway.

There was a little queue inside the toilets and everyone was talking. She tried to calm herself down by taking a deep breath. Kate closed her eyes and thought 'at least I am not alone', she could make her way to the exit when she was ready. Just then the toilet entrance door opened, she turned and looked, her eyes filled with anticipation.

"Hannah!" Kate huffed, relieved.

"Kate, what's going on? Who is that? Why did you run?" Hannah was really concerned.

"His name is Lucas, he is a very bad man, believe me… although you wouldn't believe me if I told you what he really is."

Hannah seemed confused, "Are you in trouble?" Kate looked unsure of what to say.

"I hope not Hannah. I hope not… just got to get out of here. Eve will tell you all about it, wish she was here now!" Kate shook her head, disappointed for letting herself become an easy target again.

Just then the lights and music murmured and sparked off and on, Kate looked around ready for someone to pounce on her. They all hissed off and on again, and then a sudden flash, all was dark and all was still.

"Hannah… Hannah?" Kate started to panic, it was dark and silent, and Hannah didn't answer.

Another sudden murmur and then a 'kerching' and the lights came back on. They flickered slightly and were dim, but there was still enough light to see.

Kate gasped; her face turned a pale colour. Hannah and all the other girls were frozen in time still standing where they were.

Hannah had a terrified expression on her face looking directly at Kate. Kate looked into her eyes and felt sadness build up inside her.

Two girls stood at the sinks frozen in time, they had been in the middle of a conversation whilst washing their hands. Even the water droplets hung in the air as if the whole scene were captured in a photograph.

"Kate… Oh Kate, you see I have many powers too. Come out, come out wherever you are… Ha, ha, ha…" Lucas's echoing voice mocked her as she looked around for somewhere to escape him. There was nowhere she could go. Should she just wait or try to make a run for it?

Kate moved her left hand towards the main toilet door; she placed her hand on the handle and swallowed hard wishing to herself that she could make it out. She turned and looked at Hannah, "I will come find you, I promise." Her frozen face stared back at Kate with that terrified expression, sending shivers down her spine. She turned back to face the door and opened it slightly. She peered through the crack it made, she couldn't see anyone, she took a deep breath and pulled the door open enough to slide through and make a run for it. She slid herself slowly through the crack in the doorway and turned to hold the door making sure it shut slowly and quietly behind her.

"Hello Kate." The voice echoed behind her.

Kate turned from the doorway slowly, her face filled with fear. There he stood with his hands behind his back, looking smart and smirking.

"Hello Lucas." Kate whispered under her breath.

Lucas brought his left hand forward and placed it on Kate's shoulder.

"I have not come to harm you…" His face looked concerned, but Kate knew he liked to play games.

"What do you want?" Kate's voice jerked a little as her adrenaline took hold.

"I needed to see you."

Kate pulled away from him stepping backwards.

"I know you're trying to mess with my head Lucas, it's hard to look at you after what you did to me!"

Lucas moved closer to her again and softened his voice, "I'm sorry, truly I am Kate, I thought I gave you what you wanted... I could give you so much more."

Kate narrowed her eyes, "You terrify me... Eve saved me from you and myself."

"Where is she now?"

"Trying to save others." Kate snarled.

"Kate I could tell you something that could blow your mind, just do one thing for me and I will tell you where to find your mother... I could make you so powerful!"

"I don't want to know Lucas, please just let these people go."

"One thing Kate, I just want you to do one thing."

"No! Now let them go, please!"

"Very well, I said I wouldn't harm you and I won't."

Lucas clapped his hands together and there was an almighty surge of power that triggered all the electric and people back on in one go!

"Kate!" Shouted Hannah.

Kate turned around and opened the toilet door, "There you are!" Hannah smiled.

Kate's head filled with questions and she wondered why Lucas never harmed her.

"Hannah give me a couple of secs, just need to know something."

Kate ran off through the crowds of people dancing, she looked anxiously round, but couldn't see Lucas anywhere.

"Kate!"

She spun around; Lucas stood behind her.

"Lucas, all I wanted to know was who my parents were. You gave me pain and took away my confidence. You never told me!"

Kate turned to walk away and Lucas grabbed her arm. "Vern... it's Vern. Sister Vern Smith is your mother!"

"What?! You liar!"

"Never, I owe you this much."

"But how? Why? No she would have told me!"

"That's all I know, just that she got pregnant and tried to escape it, just like you."

"What, so she became a nun and fostered me away?" Kate mocked herself at this ridiculous accusation.

"Don't know, you would have to ask your mother!"

"You're lying!"

Kate moved back into the crowd and walked towards the exit. Lucas came up behind her and whispered in her ear with his hands gently rocking her hips.

"One thing Kate, just do one thing for me."

"What do you want?"

"Tell me what she does. Tell me her weaknesses, just come to me." He smiled, he was very handsome. She turned to him.

"Betrayal! I will be betraying her and my friends." Kate looked at the floor. "No Lucas!" She turned and walked; he spun her back around and placed his hands firmly on her cheeks, but not to harm her, just to hold her still.

Lucas looked deep into her eyes, "Kate do as I ask," he demanded in a deep husky tone. He kissed her mouth as she tried to pull away, and it began, some of his energy entering her, taking over some of her thoughts.

Eve's head locked into the first memories of being awake, everyone could feel and see as her new life projected into their heads, filling them with her memories.

They saw her awake and meeting Father Josh, Vern and Kate, they felt her burning with energy. They saw her first fight with Lucas's demons outside St John's and what he had done to the poor men he had taken over. Their heads filled with the scenes of the spiritual evening and how Lucas used people's grief of dead loved ones against them. They saw all that had been happening around them without them knowing.

Eve suddenly felt a change, her thoughts spun around and she saw Kate with the others from the café. They were at a club, then she saw Lucas with Kate, he was holding her. Eve saw herself, standing with her sword held high as she plunged it into Kate.

"Argh!" Eve's eyes filled with blackness. She snapped up her hands from the earth as everyone came out of their trance.

"We have to leave!" Eve shouted to Astra, Darrel and Jin-Joel, "Something is wrong."

The people started to stand and look around at themselves and Eve.

"What are you? What do you want?" the lady at the altar said, questioning Eve as she started to walk.

"I am all of you, and I just want to lead you into the arms of our Lord."

The lady shouted after Eve as she ran towards the others, but Eve was more concerned of what she, and now a lot of others had just witnessed.

"Eve, what's wrong?" Astra asked with worried eyes.

"I just saw Kate and Lucas becoming very friendly, not sure if it's past or present with all that's going on, but we need to go and find her."

They all jumped into the car with no hesitation.

"What did you feel?" Jin-Joel asked.

"Danger, slaughter and darkness filled me; I just hope we get there in time!"

Outside the noisy club, Kate and Lucas stood in a dim lit alley. He pulled her closer towards him.

"What are you doing to me Lucas?" Kate mumbled as she tried to speak.

"Hush, I just want to make you mine." He placed his fingers on her lips. Lucas pulled Kate's head back to expose her neck. He licked and kissed her soft skin, giving her an aching pleasure. She moaned a little as he licked her lips with his tongue, rendering her powerless.

Lucas brushed her hair back with his hands then moved his hands slowly down between her breasts towards her stomach. He then spun her around so she faced the wall. Kate placed her hands out in front of her as he whispered in her ear, "is this what you want?"

Lucas kissed her softly on her back and touched her breast with his left hand.

Kate couldn't focus on anything; she wanted more, so much more. She could hear voices whispering all around her as Lucas took over.

Eve knew in her heart that she couldn't trust Kate.

"We will have to watch her… watch our backs."

"I'm sure she wouldn't turn on any of her friends Eve, you saved her life." Astra replied, trying to convince herself, if no one else.

"This is Lucas we're talking about too." Darrel looked in the rear view mirror at Astra as they pulled up to 'The Temple of Life'.

Astra and Eve rushed into 'The Temple of Life' and into the study room. Eve pushed open the bookshelf and they both rushed down the stairs.

"Kate!" Astra huffed.

Kate turned to look at them as she turned down the TV… She smiled at them both as she stretched her legs out.

"Did you get what you wanted done? How was the night?" She looked at Eve.

Eve could feel her, feel that intensity of darkness, but she smiled at Kate.

"Did you get up to much?" She asked promptly as Kate paused and stared into Eve.

"No, just hung around waiting for you guys. I've been watching a program about bugs that use other species as hosts." She smiled again at Eve and Astra.

"Kate!" Darrel sounded surprised as he walked into the room.

"Why is everyone so surprised to see me?!" Kate said in a joking tone.

"We thought you might have got bored and gone clubbing or something!" Astra looked at Eve.

"So did you get what you wanted done Eve?" Kate asked.

"For now…" Eve said as she turned towards her room.

PAST, PRESENT AND FUTURE

Eve lay on her bed wondering what to make of the whole evenings' events. Should she consult her Lord? She already knew that Kate would betray her; from the first time they met when Eve held Kate's hands and looked inside her. She wanted Kate to come and bear all so she could be rescued.

Astra lay down on her side watching her new room mate sleeping. Kate seemed so peaceful, but what did she dream? It was hard for Astra to see that soon Kate would betray them all, but how?

The morning came and she woke before Kate. She slowly got out of bed and edged her way out of the room. She knocked quietly on Eve's door.

"Eve." Astra whispered.

"Yes?" A voice came from behind her.

Eve had already been awake for hours deep in thought

"Eve I need to talk to you!" Eve lead Astra into her room.

"You want to know what we should do about Kate."

Eve sat on the bed and guided Astra with her eyes to sit down next to her.

"Yes... Eve, I can't trust her; I watched her sleeping all night long, with visions of her slitting my throat while I slept!"

Eve placed her hand on Astra's knee, "Astra that won't happen; you can always sleep in my room if you're that concerned, but we have to act like we don't know anything. If she gets any suspicions we lose her and our chance to draw in Lucas."

Astra looked into Eve's eyes, "I'm so unsure of this!"

"Don't be, you have me watching." Eve stood up, "I'm off to the gym, come with me. Here wear some of my joggers." Eve threw a pair of black jogging bottoms to Astra.

"You're right!" Astra took a deep breath and put her trust in Eve.

Later that evening as all four of them sat watching TV and eating their chicken pasta for tea they were all amused at a local story on the news.

"Lot's of strange happenings have been going on around a local cemetery, so the local vicar of the church and some of the local residents have called in a team of paranormal investigators." The newsreader then went live to a local cemetery outside North London where a man stood near a church.

Darrel and Astra looked at each other and tried not to laugh as the man spoke.

"Yes, we have been called in because local residents have seen ghostly figures and lights in the cemetery area and in the church." The man said as his raincoat swished around in the wind.

"Ghostbusters!" Darrel said and turned to Astra as a pile of food came bursting from her mouth; they stared at each other in fits of giggles.

"What's so funny?" Kate asked with a smile of her face.

"Ghostbusters!" Astra blurted.

Eve smiled as the other two had conjured up images of Ghostbusters in their vacuum cleaner outfits stalking cemeteries. What would passer's by think if they didn't know what was going on?

"They don't look like that." Kate said.

"They just take thermal meters and a psychic with them, oh yer, and a camera." Kate smiled and shook her head.

"Yes, but I like our image better." Darrel said smirking at Kate.

Wasting little time Eve opened up Darrel's laptop on the coffee table in front of her.

"Might as well look into some of the local sightings on the 'net about the strange goings on." She suggested. Walking off upstairs to the study area, Eve came across some local articles of a gliding nun who was seen by an old lady who walks her dog near by. There were a few articles on local residents seeing lights flickering in the grave yard when they had looked from their windows at night that backed onto the church grounds.

Astra walked through the sliding door in the book case.

"What do you think then?" Astra asked leaning over Eve's shoulder.

"I think someone is playing games with them all, trying to get them to believe in something that doesn't exist in real time…"

"We going to take a look tonight then?" Kate asked Darrel

"Well…" Darrel looked up from his coffee to tell Kate what he thought, but Astra interrupted as she wandered back down the metal staircase.

"Think you should stay here really Kate, it might get a bit too much, especially if Lucas is close." Astra smiled

"Oh well, I don't mind honestly, he doesn't bother me that much." Kate tried to convince them.

"No, Astra's right. You and Jin-Joel can look up more information for us while we are there and ring us if you find out anything else." Darrel suggested; his eyebrows drew upwards and he looked at Eve seeking her approval as she stood at the top of the staircase looking down at them all. "Sounds like a good idea to me," Eve said looking at Kate trying to read her thoughts.

Eve sat back down in the study room on the nice dark brown leather desk chair. She soon came across an article of the ghost hunters coming to town. There was a picture attached to the article entitled "Ted and his Ghost Hunters Come to Town". In the picture Ted the Paranormal Investigator stood with the local Vicar in the church grounds with some grave stones around them.

Something caught Eve's eye as she looked a little closer, she noticed a name on the grave stone to the right of the picture. 'Anna Howard, a loving woman to all who knew her'. Eve's heart skipped a beat, her mind crashed for a second inside. Suddenly memories of Christine's life ran through her brain.

Christine's mother's words rang through her head, and pictures filled her brain of someone caring and loving; always picking her up after a fall.

A small brunette lady, with pretty brown eyes smiled at her.

Eve gasped and opened her eyes, she stood up in shock. 'Could this be Christine's mother, her real mother?' She closed her eyes again and thought to herself, 'I have to let it go!', but she wanted to know more, she had an urging feeling inside to know.

Eve wanted to investigate the paranormal site before they went later that evening, but she wanted to go alone for now. She was unsure of what her feelings would hold, and if she went with the others they might see a side of her that could leave her weak and she definitely didn't want Kate knowing her thoughts and feelings! This was wrong wanting to know, but she needed to know before they investigated together.

"Darrel." Eve said as she joined the others in the living area. Darrel looked up with a slight start.

"What's the matter gorgeous?" He said with a chuckle.

"Can I have the keys to the car?"

"Going somewhere?" He asked as Astra looked slightly surprised.

"Thought I might check out the paranormal area on my own to see if I can pick up anything!"

"Ok, here…" He said passing the keys and a rough guide map of how to get there.

"You gonna be alright finding your way?" Astra asked.

"If I get stuck I will ring you from the car." Eve said picking up Darrel's phone from the coffee table.

Silence passed in Eve's thoughts as she passed through London City, there were no real thoughts that were really there, no big emotions or notions filled her and why should they? She could barely remember Christine's past memory. It was curiosity more than anything that grabbed her attention now, not the shock of thinking her birth mother could be dead and buried.

Eve looked up at the church as she parked on the street outside, it was not hard to find. Right outside the church gates, TV crews were packing up and others were unpacking equipment ready for any footage that they could capture tonight at the paranormal investigation.

There was a slight breeze outside, Eve zipped up her jacket. She walked on passed the smaller gate to the right of the church, the path led round to the back where there was a little entrance to the big grave filled cemetery. Eve aimed her way towards to big tree on her left near the bottom of the grave yard; she had noticed the big tree beside the two men in the picture she had looked at earlier. Studying the marked stones with her eyes she noticed first her birth fathers grave, 'John Howard Suddenly Taken From Us'. Eve felt a deep inner turmoil, emotions grabbed her as she saw her mothers stone. She had fallen asleep two years previous, 2008. 'Anna Howard, loving wife, mother and grandmother'. Grandmother! Eve's eyes found Christine's pain, "Mum" she gasped, she bent down at some old dry flowers on the grave, running her fingers down her mother's headstone, she whispered, "Won't be long and I will see you again." Eve thought of judgement day, when everyone would rise from their sleep. A grabbing pain and shock made her stand suddenly, her eyes widened at the stone beside her mother, 'Christine Anna Clover, May God Rest Her Soul in Pure Love. Great loving wife and mother'. She tried to shake off her feelings. She remembered her baby, "I can't be here" she said under her breath. Maybe it had been a bad idea for her to come, for whatever reason she thought. She turned away and thought about what she was fighting for; she was fighting for love, justice and to stop all of this pain.

Eve closed her eyes and faced towards the sunlight, "Forgive me my Lord for wondering, please help me be stronger so I may not get lost." She swallowed hard and started to walk away, back down the path that led back to the car. Being there had answered what she wanted and now she must return and never think of it again, Christine's life.

As she reached the entrance back to the church ground she could hear a pair of foot steps coming towards her. As Eve passed the entrance a young lad in his early teens went to walk past her. They grabbed each others gaze as he brushed his way past. Green eyes and wavy dark blonde hair… "SNAP!" A sharp electrical pulse spun into Eve, she lowered her head and kept walking. Her heart pumped so hard she heard it in her ears. She heard his foot steps stop on the small gravel path. The young lad turned as Eve kept walking.

"Christine!" He raised his voice – directed at her. Eve closed her eyes for a second and thought, 'NO!'

"Mum!" He shouted. Eve stopped sharp, breathed in, and then kept walking.

She quickly started up the engine and noticed a mountain bike chained at the big gate to the church yard.

On the way back she denied all to herself and felt a big trip of guilt. She could feel a travelling stranger following her moves, but saw nothing around her apart from the hustle of people on the streets.

She arrived back at home and did not say a word to the others about what had happened. She needed to speak to the spirit council; she felt a big feeling of need. "I'm off to the shower." She said to them.

"Ok? Is all ok with you?" Darrel said puzzled as she didn't seem herself.

"Yes, just need some me time." She declared as she closed the bathroom door.

Eve turned on the shower, she got undressed and stepped into the spraying water. As the steam grew thicker she closed her eyes and opened herself to a meditation state.

"I need to talk Lord, God, Father."

The sound of the water drifted away. As she opened her eyes they filled with white light. She saw four figures standing around her; she walked closer to the centre of them, the steam cleared. Grass lay beneath her and stones stood 12ft high on the grassland all around her. Eve spoke into the air, "I crossed the line… I entered Christine's world and I believe I might have disturbed things around us and feelings hidden in me."

A strong male voice came from the stone shadows as the figure emerged. "Eve it was never going to be easy, but to walk into Christine's life was an unnecessary risk and now you could collide your two beings and bring

heartache to yourself, which could have devastating consequences and leave you open to Lucas and the other demons you will eventually meet."
"I know… I fell!" Eve bowed her head.
Archangel Uriel stood in front of her.
"Be more wise, you have the key to this, Eve stand with strength… you will soon reach a crossroads with a choice to make." The young looking Archangel placed his hand on her shoulder. Her body filled with strength, she gasped and closed her eyes as the light and energy absorbed her entirely. She floated up into the air covered in a white beaming protective glow. It felt like her whole being was being taken apart piece by piece and then placed back together – brand new.
Eve opened her eyes; water poured all over her back and she felt she was in full control of all and everything to come.

Outside 'The Temple of Life' on the street a black and silver mountain bike skidded to a halt. The young lad on the bike looked up at the building; he had seen Eve go inside and wanted to know more. He was so sure he recognised her.
He stepped off his bike, maybe it was his adrenaline taking over, but he was very sure he needed to knock on the wooden door in front of him. 'BANG, BANG, BANG, BANG', the door seemed to echo. He looked on the floor and back in front again. It seemed to takes ages before an answer came. The door opened and the young lad swallowed hard. Jin-Joel stood in the doorway and smiled.
"Hi there have you come to find out about our training programs?"
"Erm… Well no… I actually came here to find someone. I'm looking for a lady called Christine, I'm sure I saw her come here." The lads' voice became more confident.
"I don't know anyone here named Christine, maybe an Astra, Kate or Eve? There's definitely no Christine." Jin-Joel answered slightly puzzled.
"No, no, definitely Christine I was looking for."
Jin-Joel looked a little confused at the young lad, "Can I take your name, and I'll ask the girls if they know anything." That's all Jin-Joel could say to him.
"Yes, my name is Michael Clover; I'm staying at Privilege Foster Home at the moment, if you hear anything…"
"We will get in contact if we know anything, Michael Clover?"
"Yes, that's it, thanks, thanks." Michael raised a hand to say a friendly goodbye, but he was still sure she was there.

Jin-Joel shut the door and turned around, Astra stood behind him.
"Did I hear him right? The young lad is Michael, Christine's son?" Astra
sounded shocked.
"Yes you heard right, we must talk to Eve!"
"But how did he know, how has this happened?" Puzzled, they made
their way to the living area.

"Eve, we might have a bit of a problem." Astra said as Eve looked up
from the kitchen work surface, her palms were flat on the surface and she
took a deep breath.
"A young lad followed me home, Michael... Christine's son!"
Eve looked into Astra's eyes as she nodded slowly with an anxious look.
"What?!" Darrel stared up in slight shock from the sofa.
"So what happens now?" Astra asked, also knowing the others had the
same question on their minds.
"We just go on with things and do what we do best, I will challenge the
situation as and when it arrives." Eve said with a slight coldness in her
voice.
Darrel, Astra and Jin-Joel all looked at each other.
"Eve!" Astra tried to place a hand on Eve's, but she pulled away.
"Astra, I know what needs to be done." She smiled and walked towards
the sofa with a cup of tea. As she sat down and sipped from the cup Kate
slowly closed Astra's bedroom door from where she had been listening.

Later that evening the gang assembled some night goggles and torches
together, Darrel placed a hand gun in his bag too, he wanted to risk
nothing tonight.
"Is this a good idea tonight Eve, I mean with today's shocker and where
we are going!" Astra said as she looked up from her bag.
"It's got to be done, and yes it is ok." Eve pulled her black bag onto her
back.
They all snapped on their seat belts and made their way to the cemetery.
Darrel didn't notice the silver mountain bike in the shadows following
them, but Eve felt it, like wind playing in her hair, it can't be seen, but
you know it is there.
As they arrived at the cemetery, the paranormal investigators were still
setting up their equipment, both in the cemetery and on top of their van
parked outside. They were testing different angles to try and get the best
footage from the recording equipment in the van. Spectators had started

to arrive, but a small group of people were telling them to stay back a bit as they may interrupt the equipment.

Eve and the others sat in their vehicle watching and waiting for the evenings' activities to start.

"Well at least if people do see or find anything we can step in and show them what's really going on." Astra said.

"The fight for followers." Darrel jested slightly.

"No, I meant that what we see isn't always real!" Astra pointed out, unamused.

"The dead don't walk." Darrel said.

"I wouldn't be too sure… I walk." Eve smiled.

"What do you think they will find Eve?" Astra asked.

"Maybe kids messing around, I'm not sure my feelings were a bit messed up earlier. If it's Lucas's workings, I would expect a great show to try and tell the nation lies about the afterlife."

Darrel rubbed his face, Astra stared all around from the car window and Eve felt surges of adrenaline as she knew in one way or another there would be confrontation tonight.

Chssss… "Is all well?" Jin-Joel came over the radio in the car.

"All well Jin-Joel, we will be moving in shortly." Darrel said as he held the microphone to his lips.

"Keep in touch." Jin-Joel said as the voice hissed away.

All the equipment seemed to be set as three men climbed in to the back of the black van. Now it was just a wait to see if anything would unfold. Time seemed to tick away slowly, as they all tried to wait patiently in the dark. It seemed hours, but it was only two that had gone by. The clock in the car read 10:16pm when Darrel sat up sharp.

"Sure, I just saw a flash of light!"

"Yes, there it is again." Astra whispered with slight excitement.

"A glowing from behind the church." Eve pointed out.

"Let's quietly jump over the short wall in front and make our way round the back." Eve said.

"Keep close to the church wall on the left side so we don't have to pass the black van." Darrel instructed.

All three crept from the car and quietly made their way over the flint wall, so as not to be seen they all crouched low and moved towards the left side of the church.

Seeing lights glowing from the back of the church, all three slowly moved towards them.

"Wonder what they can see on their equipment?" Astra whispered.

"Oh wow." Darrel stood with his mouth open wide as they all saw bright white balls of light dancing around the cemetery. The light looked a bit like the energy Eve could muster up when needed for protection. Eve's heart pounded, she could feel electrical impulses all around her. People were looking from their windows from the houses that backed onto the church grounds.

They all suddenly heard voices coming towards them from the right side of the church. All three in their dark clothes backed into the church's shadows and watched.

A television camera made its entrance with a man carrying it crouching down, while another man held a microphone in his hand and a lady dressed in a dark dress was talking.

"Hi, I'm Janice a psychic medium." She announced walking on, she then stopped and raised her right arm directing the camera.

"If you can see this, it is fantastic and we are going to try and make some contact tonight with these spirits." She claimed.

Eve looked on and shook her head, 'Will they never learn?' she thought to herself.

"Fantastic, fantastic!" Janice said as they watched the light show. Janice closed her eyes and touched her temples. The camera panned around her as she made ridiculous noises.

"Oh, umm, I'm trying to make contact, oh yes, oh one of the spirits is coming into contact, oh yes it's a young child. Ah bless her, she is saying it's time to play, we have come to play." She said still with her eyes closed and looking like someone trying to make sense of the madness.

Eve had already had enough! She grabbed Astra's arm.

"That's enough." She said loudly.

"What a load of nonsense, you want to see what these creatures really are then I'll show you." Eve said as she turned her gaze from the 'actress' to the light show.

"How dare you insult me…" She shouted at Eve, "Cut the film, CUT THE FILM!" She screamed at the camera man. "Who the hell do you think you are!" She demanded to know.

Eve looked back at her as Darrel and Astra stood either side of her. Eve turned back to the lights and announced herself.

"I am Eve, daughter of the heavens, bringer of life, death and justice to all who live among us – light and dark. I am a protector of God's throne and a saviour to all his people, and I ask these strange lights to announce themselves and to show us their true form."

Eve's eyes filled with light and the wind grew round the trees swaying them from side to side.

"You're mad, absolutely insane." The woman mocked.

Eve turned towards Janice and her camera crew, her eyes glowing with white light as she placed a finger on her lips to silence her.

"Shh! Watch this…" She said softly.

"Oh. My. GOD!" Janice gasped in shock.

"Role it, record it!" The man with the microphone shouted as the wind crept amongst them.

The lights started getting wilder, and whizzing around; one hovered over the camera and then suddenly shot down at the two men.

"Leave them!" Astra shouted.

The ball of light then went to target Astra; she turned completely to face it. The light shot up into the air and then shot down at her, she closed her eyes as it tried to make contact. Eve spun around and caught it in her hand before it hit Astra. Eve crushed it and it burst into more balls of light.

"Stand behind me." She instructed to her friends. She raised her hands up from her body as light glowed inside and now all around her body.

"I demand in the name of the Lord of Light to announce yourselves." She demanded again.

This time she brought the wind at them, throwing them up into the air and twisting them around in small circles.

One by one each light ball burst, creating yet more light. They whizzed around at each other as a green mist grew around the cemetery. As it grew thicker the light balls shot into each other, and disappeared into the mist.

It grew so thick, Astra and Darrel, started to become alarmed.

"Stay where you are, all together, don't move, that's what it wants, to target you one by one." Eve spoke out of the mist.

"I can't see you Eve!" Darrel said softly.

"I'm here…" Astra said.

Dark shadowed figures formed in the mist in front of them all.

"What are they?!" Astra whispered concerned.

"We're gonna find out!" Eve said.

The mist started to lift slightly and the figures emerged from it.

"Zombies!" Janice cried out.

"Don't run." Eve shouted, "They are feeding on your fear."

"We are gonna have to fight," said Eve to her two friends.

A hand approached Eve from out of the mist; she grabbed it and pulled it towards her.

"Mum." It was Michael. Eve looked alarmed at him.

"What! You! Get back!" she pushed him behind her as a zombie's arm came through the mist.

"Eve closed her eyes, "Wind!" she brought the breeze and it started blowing through the mist. She grabbed at the blood drenched scabby arm and pulled it toward her as the wind caught hold and dispersed the mist. The zombie took the form of Christine's mother. "Come to me my baby", she lurched from behind Eve at Michael.

"Is that Nan?" Michael squealed.

"No, they're feeding from your emotions and fears."

Eve kicked the disgusting creature backwards. As it came at them again she took her sword from her side and swiped off its head.

Eve looked around as Darrel pinned a zombie on the floor with his foot and shot it in the head. Blood spurted up the side of Janice's face.

"Argh! I want to get out of here!" She cried into her hands in desperation.

Astra ran up behind Darrel as a blood drenched zombie carrying an axe took a swipe at her. BANG! Darrel shot it in the head, and it dropped to the floor.

"I was just thinking about them zombie games we used to play Darrel, never thought I'd see one for real!" Astra admitted.

"What do we do?" Cried the cameraman as the wind started to roar.

"Stand behind me!" Eve demanded.

The flesh decaying zombies stood back up and changed back into balls of light, they merged into one big ball of light.

Eve summoned her energy, her light energy grew more intense and swirls of light moved all around her.

The big ball shifted into another figure, it looked like Eve, and it walked towards the real Eve.

Its eyes were filled with darkness and hate. As it got closer licks of fire grew outwards from it, twisting and turning all around it. It drew a sword up into the air and let out a high pitch squeal as it ran towards Eve.

"NO!" Michael shouted as Darrel held both his arms back to stop him running in.

Eve's sword charged with light as she sharply sprung it out in front of her.

"Arrrgggghhh!!!" The beast shrieked in pain as the sword plunged into its torso. The beast stumbled back off the blade and laughed, until it looked down, then the laughter soon turned to panic. White light seeped out from the hole the blade had made, it held its stomach and looked at Eve.

"Sleep now!" She said as the beasts body cracked like a sheet glass; light filled every crack.

Eve held her arm up into the air as the beast let out one last shriek and shattered with an explosion into the night air.

"Demons." Eve huffed as she brushed some demon dust off her shoulder and the light energy seeped back inside her body.

Darrel helped Janice up off the floor as three more men from the van ran towards them to see all the commotion.

"Did you get any of that?" Astra mocked

Janice stood with her mouth open as did the others.

"It's blank, all blank!" The cameraman said as he searched through the film on his camera.

"Let's go," said Darrel.

Eve looked at Michael, he was white with shock, "It's over, it's ok we can take you home," she said placing a hand on his arm.

"I… I don't understand what's happening." He gasped.

"Balance between good and evil." Eve said sternly.

"Thought that was just fairy-tales." Said the cameraman.

"Tell people what you saw tonight… demons playing games, wanting to distract you from the truth." Eve said to them all.

"What is the truth." Murmured Janice.

"That death is death, eternal sleep until judgement is made on the earth, listening to voices in your head will only lead to self-destruction." Eve spoke looking at each of them.

Darrel placed a hand on Eve's shoulder, "Time to go."

As they left they looked up at the people in their windows who had witnessed most of the evenings' activities and Eve hoped they had learnt a great lesson; nothing is quite as it seems. If it seems too good to be true, it usually is.

"More followers for us I hope." Darrel said as they walked away.

As they all climbed into the car a voice sounded out from the night. It was the cameraman's assistant, he ran up to the car window as Darrel was about to reverse.

"Wait, what if someone wants to interview you about tonight? Wait, Eve!" He sounded off as they pulled away.

"Are you my mum?" Michael asked Eve as they sat in the back of the car together.

"Michael, I was once Christine Clover yes, but she died and I was then resurrected as Eve – the bringer of judgement and light." Eve held his hand.

"I don't understand… Why were you resurrected? It seems so surreal." Michael started to sound anxious and confused.

"Hush. Calm down! It does take you time to get your head around it." Astra turned and placed a hand on his knee, "Judgement Day is coming Michael, and all that sleeps will be woken to walk the earth once more. When the fallen angels, the demons awake they will destroy everything that is not protected. God our Lord needed a bringer of light on the earth. Eve is here to help people believe before all is woken, so everyone who believes and repents is protected by the Lord of Lights' Sword of Justice, while the demons try and destroy the earth. Everyone will stand before our Lord in judgement even the evil among us. Our Lord of Light will then destroy the fallen angels and their demonic followers forever and then the earth will be wiped clean."

Eve looked at Michael for a reaction.

"Peace on earth…" He whispered.

"But why you, why my mother?" He asked unsure.

"Christine made the ultimate sacrifice of saving her son… you. Without any hesitation she gave up her own life to save yours, it made her pure and that's what was needed to resurrect the light to begin what is happening now." Eve grabbed both of Michael's hands.

"You still remember me though don't you?" Michael said with humble emotion in his voice.

"Yes I do, you gave me that memory back when we passed at the cemetery earlier." Eve answered truthfully.

"I'll call you Eve." He looked up; his eyes glazed over with emotions.

"You need to sleep." Eve said softly.

"Is this it? The road you live on." Darrel said as they came to a road slightly run down and dimly lit.

"Yes." He said, "Eve can I see you tomorrow please?"

"Well, yes you can but it might be a good idea to give us both a little time to adjust." She answered, "I don't recognise this place!" She continued.

"No, no we moved." Michael said abruptly.

Darrel moved his bike from out of the car and gave it to Michael.
"Thanks... see you later." He said as he waved a hand into the air.
"You ok?" Astra said as they drove home.
"Yes, I suppose I am." Eve smiled.

Morning came and the entire house woke for breakfast. One by one, Eve,
Astra, Darrel and Kate made their way to the sofa with coffee.
"So what happened last night? You didn't say much when you got
home." Kate said.
"The usual!" Astra said wisely wiping her eyes. There was a thick feeling
in the air that morning. Michael was not on the agenda for discussing
whilst Kate was present. Darrel flicked on the local morning news.
"Hey, hey there it is!" He said with amusement looking at the television.
A reporter from the news was talking over some footage from the
investigation and episodes that happened the previous night.
All you could see was lights flashing in the green mist, then as the mist
cleared you could just make out Eve plunging her sword into the demon,
then an explosion of dust as it shattered into the air.
"A fantastic light show for us if I must say so myself, but in the real scope
of things we knew from what we have heard and seen from last nights'
activities that something is amiss here. People are discussing the issues of
angels and demons. Apparently the woman in the footage is Eve and
believes herself to be the bringer of peace. Well that's to be seen, but
from what we heard from our investigation team this was a real event that
took place last night."
The lady reporter stopped talking and the others stopped staring at the
screen and then turned to each other.
"Fantastic!" Astra said out loud, "At least they got some footage then."

Two weeks past by as they all decided to keep a low profile for a while,
outside in the city the air was growing much cooler; autumn was
definitely on the way. Rain began to gather in the clouds above as a
mountain bike raced up the road towards 'The Temple of Life', the bike
shuddered to a halt and Michael jumped off.
'KNOCK, KNOCK' the wooden door echoed down the hallway.
"Michael!" Darrel said surprised as he opened the door.
"Can I speak to you all?" He asked in an uncertain voice.
"Yes, yes wait in the study, I will go and get Eve." Darrel answered,
pointing his hand towards the study area on the right.

"Thanks." Michael said as he unbuttoned his coat.

Darrel walked into the gym. Eve was sat in meditation thinking of the night at the cemetery.

Eve already knew Michael was there and opened her eyes as Darrel walked towards her.

"Michael…" She nodded at Darrel, "it's ok I will go and see him."

"Yer." Darrel said as he scrunched up his eyes realising that not a lot gets past Eve.

Eve flung a small white towel over her shoulder and sipped from a glass of water as she made her way across the gym towards the door.

Michael was sitting down and swiverling the chair in the study from side to side as Eve walked in.

"Hi." Eve said with a smirk.

"Hi." Michael smiled brushing down the top of his hair with his hand.

"Erm, Eve, I came to see you and… well I wanted to know a little more about what is happening." He looked at her for some sort of support.

"I see, you want to get to know about the unseen goings on here on our planet?" Eve smiled.

"Well yer, it's just some of it is a little hard to take in… I mean last night I read about Adam and Eve and well, it just seems a bit too far fetched to me. Is it true?" Michael frowned at Eve a little.

"That story is what you want it to be, there's a lot of morals to learn from that story. Jealously, greed, selfishness, not trusting in yourself, biting the hand that feeds you, I could go on!" Eve looked into his eyes.

"Is it true?" Michael questioned her.

"It's what you want to believe Michael, and it all depends on what story you've read, I can tell you the story I know." Eve suggested.

"So what's happening now? Why is this all happening?" Michael looked intensely at Eve for answers.

"At this present moment, most of the fallen angels cast out from heaven that changed the earth hundreds of years ago are banished and bound under the earth waiting for judgement. They are slowly stirring from there sleep.

Lucas is a demon and a son of these fallen angels and he walks the earth turning people. He promises them there desires but really they are damaging themselves and others in many ways, through the things they believe will bring them love, money, peace and balance in their lives.

Lucas and his many helpers hate us, hate the earth all because they are jealous of why it was made and that the 'Lord of Light' loves us because we are part of him and he offers us forgiveness, but the fallen will be in torment for their sins forever. They have been forsaken by the heavens and can never return. It's a fight to gain as many followers as we can so human life can live with rule and harmony.

Eve looked at Michael with concerning eyes and wondered if that information was a little too overwhelming for him.
"So is it a good or a bad thing with me around?" He asked, concerned.
"It's not the best idea, no! But I will protect you if that's what you want."
Eve blinked and pondered on what he had said. Michael looked down and studied his hands.
"Michael, can I try something on you?" Eve asked.
"Like what?" Michael's voice sounded unsure.
"If I want I can see your past and some of your future if you let me?"
Eve wanted to know a little more herself and things seemed a little unsettled within him.
"I… I don't know if you will like what you see," he said as Eve walked towards him.
"Let me see Michael." Eve asked. A light started to burn within her eyes and she held out her hand. A snap and a crack hit the air as their minds connected.
Eve could see Christine's death once again, her blood trickling from her body on to the road, the two boys in the car that hit her had horror written all over their faces.
She saw her funeral and Jake, Michael's father and Christine's husband breaking inside. 'SNAP, CRACK' time then whizzed on to Jake going off in anger on his bike as Michael peeped from his grandmother's front door.
"I can't do this." Michael spurted out as he pulled away from Eve.
"It's ok; just tell me when you're ready." Eve said wiping away the tears that ran down Michael's face. Eve knelt in front of him and held him close.
"When you, well mum died dad went a bit crazy and went looking for the boys that ran mum down. They tried to run from the accident, they were joy riders. Dad found them and beat them within an inch of their lives. The police arrested him at the scene." Michael sniffed and looked at Eve.
"So what happened to you?" Eve asked concerned.
"Well the boys got seven years each for dangerous driving and for running away from the scene of the accident. They got a further seven

years for manslaughter charges. Dad got twelve months for ABH on the boys. He was out within six months for compassion and good behaviour, but that was just the start of things."

"So where is your father now?" Eve asked.

"Well I went to live with nan until dad came home but he started going out drinking and fighting. He just drinks now." Michael looked up at Eve, "As for me I'm living in care hoping one day he will listen to me and help himself, cos I need him!" Michael waited for an answer from Eve, but she was trying hard to hide how she was feeling, angry and hurt for Michael.

"Michael, where is your dad now?" She asked sharply.

"Still at home probably, drinking his life away."

Eve shook her head, she stood up and paced around.

"Show me!" She ordered.

"You can't go banging on the door, imagine what he will think!" Michael's voice filled with anxiety.

"SHOW ME!" Eve raised her voice.

GONE TOO FAR?

Tania-Jane

"You can't go there Eve." Jin-Joel held his arm against the front door to the temple.

"Please Jin-Joel move out of the way." Eve said soft but sternly.

"You will be breaking the trust and rule of being here. Think about what will happen if Lucas finds Christine's past, he will use her old life against you." Jin-Joel sounded very stern, but in a caring tone. Eve turned around and looked at Michael.

"Jin-Joel is right, he is, but I can't let Christine's old life become nothing. Michael needs his father… come on." She grabbed Michael's arm and Jin-Joel moved out of the way shaking his head at her.

The car slowed up at a nice little road from a nicely kept housing estate. "There, that's the one." Michael said pointing to a house with a shabby looking front garden and a peeling blue front door.

"Ok let's see if anyone is home." Eve said stepping from the drivers' side of the car. Leaves rustled passed her black boots as memories grabbed her attention. In her mind the front lawn was pond shaped with small bushes under the window. The driveway was paved to the left and on the driveway stood an old black Suzuki motorbike, the engine still warm and an oily smell filled her senses.

"Eve!" Michael said as he stood in front of her. She blinked her eyes and came back to reality. Leaves blew across the overgrown lawn and the bushes had started to cover the front window.

"You ready?" Eve asked Michael as she placed a hand on his shoulder.

"I think so. Don't knock, it's ok I still have a key." He swiftly announced. Michael placed the key in the lock and pushed the door open.

"Oh!" Eve said as she placed a hand over her nose, "Smells of dirty ashtrays." She said as she kicked a pile of junk mail away from the door. The dining room was to the right and the sitting room to the left. It was dark in the house, all the curtains were closed.

"Let's open some curtains and windows." Eve said.

She walked into the sitting room; there were empty cans of lager everywhere. She opened the curtains and the window facing the front lawn. The sitting room looked a lot lighter, but needed a damn good clean. The dust hit the light from the window and shimmered as it found a place to start to settle once more.

"Eve!" Michael's voice came from the dining room.

Eve walked over to see the dining table pushed against the wall near the window and a couch filled with something nearly living in the middle of the room.

Michael looked at Eve, "So what now?" he whispered.

"Jake, hey you Jake, wake up!" Eve kicked over some cans laying in the middle of the floor.

"Hey you!" She shouted.

"W-w-what, I told you I'll give you the money tomorrow." He murmured.

"Jake get up now!" Eve screamed into his face, as he opened his eyes and faced himself looking straight up at her.

His eyes were red and blood-shot, his dark curtain parted hair looked wet with sweat and his face was starting to grow a forest. He wore a grubby white t-shirt that looked like it had not been washed for a year and his denim jeans had seen better days that was for sure.

He blinked his brown eyes and tried to adjust to the light. He sat up and rubbed his eyes with his right finger and thumb.

"Michael, Michael, what are you doing here?" Jake said focussing; still half cut on alcohol.

"What you doing here? Nice to see you're sober I might add!" Eve said in a sarcastic, yet angry tone.

"What!!! Who the hell do you think… Christine?!" Jake said looking puzzled and concerned with Eve standing over him, "I'm dreaming, or seeing things cos you look just like my wife." He laughed.

"Dad I needed to talk to you." Michael said moving closer.

Jake stood up and slowly staggered to the kitchen.

"Gotta get a glass of water." He murmured.

"Maybe that's what you should stay on from now onwards, don't you think Jake?" Eve said as she walked up behind him.

"Who do you think you are? You're not my wife, get out of my house!"

"No! Oh, I'm not going anywhere, this ends now. Christine is dead Jake, but Michael is here and he needs you!"

"You don't know anything about it!" Jake spoke in an aggressive tone as he put down the glass and walked over to the fridge. He opened the fridge door and took out a couple of cans of lager and stumbled back to the dining room.

"Dad please, I just want to talk to you." Michael insisted.

"I can't you remind me of your mother, just go and take that bitch with you!" His voice raised in volume, with more male arrogance to it.

As Jake sat back down on the sofa, Eve snatched the cans from his hand. "I said this ends now Jake, you need to get yourself sorted." She insisted. Jake stood back up and Michael's eyes filled with tears.

"Give 'em back now bitch!" He demanded.

"Oh I'll give you something." Eve said.

He lunged at her to grab the cans and Eve pushed him backwards. He stumbled slightly then tried to slap her face. Eve grabbed his arm and twisted it behind him and bent him over the sofa.

"Get off me!" He screamed out.

"Not yet." She said as she placed a hand on his head, "Shh… sleep now." She whispered into his ear.

Jake suddenly became limp all over his body. Eve dragged him back onto the sofa so he was lying down once again.

"Eve what are you going to do to him?" Michael asked, a little worried.

"Make him sober, make him better." Eve said stroking Jakes hair away from his face.

"Michael, get rid of all the cans in the house please and I will rescue your father while he sleeps." She assured him.

Michael started to collect the cans in boxes that lay around the house as Eve watched Jake breathing for a second.

Eve grabbed hold of his t-shirt and ripped it open to display his bare chest. She place one hand over his solar-plexus and one hand on the brow of his head.

Eve's eyes filled with white light, while white ghostly light started moving from her solar-plexus expanding out like a shield covering her whole being. Eve sunk within herself and asked for the help of healing. Her emotions filled with harmony and thoughts of a white dancing presence casting out darkness.

The light energy now seeped from, and over her whole body, it channelled its way from her, down her kneeling body, through her hands into and over Jake.

Jakes body lay with complete stillness and his breathing deepened as the healing light took hold. It seeped into him, his eyes and mouth glowing, and as more burning white light seeped over his body it glittered with gold.

"Release the darkness." Eve spoke out in a deep echoed voice that didn't seem like her at all.

Michael now stood back by the window and was watching in great amazement. Jake's head tilted backwards and his lungs took an enormous breath inwards.

"Release the darkness!" Eve demanded in that deep hypnotic tone. Jake's eyes and mouth opened wide.

"Arrrggghhh..." he shouted out as beads and beams of black negative energy spurted out of his body. Out from his eyes and mouth, gushing darkness spread out above him.

Jake took his final gasp for air as his eyes closed once more and he fell into a deep sleep again. The dark beams of smoky light were soon overtaken and eaten by Eve's burning white shadow of light.

The light now gathered and drained back into Jakes body, healing his whole being. Eve took her hands away from his body and took two deep breaths. She stroked his head and looked within herself hoping she would dissolve any old feelings away, so there were no risks to any of them.

"Eve is he ok?" Michael whispered.

"Yes, just let him sleep it off. We should wait with him a while." Eve said standing up and covering Jake with a blanket. "He will be ok, I promise." She added reassuringly.

"So while we wait shall we try cleaning up a bit more?" Michael asked.

"Why not." Eve smiled.

As late afternoon came and the sun was falling, Jake started to stir from his sleep. Eve placed a glass of water and a plate of toast beside him on a little coffee table that had been hidden out of the way before now.

"Hi." Eve said softly as Jake opened his eyes.

"Hi, am I still dreaming?" Jake asked.

"No, no dad it's ok." Michael suddenly said as Jake started to sit up.

"Christine?" Jake murmured.

"No, I'm Eve; I just came to see how you are!"

"Well I... I feel quite good actually." Jake said with a surprised tone in his voice.

"Well you eat something and get yourself smartened up and we can have a little chat." Eve announced.

"Well ok, but what about?"

"I'll explain everything soon and maybe I can show you something you may need to understand too!" As Eve spoke she turned to look at Michael and gave him a little smile.

Eve and Michael carried on cleaning up the house, Eve threw washing into the washing machine as Jake went upstairs to freshen himself up.

Jake came down the stairs still a little damp from his shower.
"Phew, I do feel better after that. You know, you do look like Christine; I can't help staring, sorry. I know she would be looking a little older by now though." Jake smiled at Eve as she sat on the sofa. The house looked and smelt a lot cleaner than it did before.
"Jake, what do you remember about earlier?" Eve asked.
"Not much to be honest, everything is usually a blur. I didn't know you and Michael were here!" Jake answered truthfully.
"Jake I need to show you something and explain some things to you, although it may be hard to take in." Eve tried to explain.
Jake walked over and sat down next to her, "What's the matter?" he asked concerned.
"First I want your promise… No more drink and just please look after Michael." She said pleading.
"Yes, I really mean it, I know it's hard, but I am gonna try alright!"
"Good." Eve said in an eerie tone as she grabbed his hand.

In a flash, they were back at Eve's resurrection and event by event she showed him her new reality. Then her voice swamped his mind, telling him how Christine's death was a key to open the door to Eve.

Jake pulled away from Eve and looked straight at her.
"I don't know what to say or what to think. This is too surreal, I'm sorry." Jake held his hand across his mouth in deep thought and walked away upstairs. Eve wasn't too sure how he was going to feel.

"Eve, I rang the foster home on my mobile and told them I was staying here for a couple of days, as dad is ill. They're not too happy, but they agreed as long as I ring them first thing in the morning," Michael said walking through to the sitting room, "Where's dad?"
"He has gone to think upstairs, I tried to explain a few things to him and he's trying to take it in." She explained.
"Michael, when you get the chance find out about how your dad is feeling."
"Yes I will do." Michael assured her.

"I have to go before it gets too much later, but give it a few days and let me know what's happening, ok?"

"Ok, yer, sure… and Eve, thank you." Michael said pleased.

Eve cuddled him and then turned away to go home, ignoring any awkward feelings.

CHANGE IS FOR THE GOOD?

Eve dreamt of falling, falling through space and time, not knowing how to stop. Air whizzed passed her ears and echoes of previous conversations were all around her.

Eve woke abruptly as she fell out of bed. Astra ran into her room.

"Eve you ok?" She asked watching Eve pick herself up from the floor.

"Well that's never happened before!" She giggled looking at Astra's face as she beamed a smile back. Astra stepped further into Eve's room and perched herself on the side of the bed.

"Eve, erm… I know you haven't said much about what's happening with Michael, but we were just wondering if everything is ok."

"Sorry, yes, I'm fine. I'm hoping Jake; his father sorts himself out so they can both get their lives back on track together again… I'm actually waiting to hear some news." Eve said happily and honestly.

"Ok, but I just want you to know, we will always trust in what you do… I think we might have a problem coming with Kate… She has been sneaking out at night!" Astra said like it was burning her up inside.

"I had actually noticed, was gonna follow her myself tonight to see what's going on!" Eve promised as she stood up and walked towards the bedroom door. "My stomach needs food," Eve placed a hand on her tummy and walked towards the kitchen.

"Eve, Martin is on the phone, it sounds urgent!" Darrel walked over with the mobile home phone.

"Hi Martin, what's wrong?"

"Hi. Is everything ok up there? It's just Kate left a message last night telling me Father Josh needs to come see you, and she also said she didn't want to see me anymore."

"Martin, I'm now totally confused myself. Let me have a long chat with Kate and I will call you back… ok?"

"Yes, yes ok… will be waiting." Martin said confused.

"Kate…" Eve knocked on the bathroom door.

The door opened and steam hit the cool air, "What's the matter?" She asked innocently.

"I think we need to have a little chat, don't you?" Eve said strictly with a hint of concern.

Eve followed Kate into Astra's room. She flung a damp towel on the floor and started brushing her damp hair with Astra's brush.

"What's the matter then?" She said in a slightly rude tone looking at Eve's reflection as she talked.

"Well apparently you left a very confusing message on Martin's phone last night."

"Yes I did, I don't want to be with him anymore, it's not doing much for me." Kate tried to ignore Eve's stare.

"What about Father Josh? You wanted to see him, or said I did... So what's your answer for that?" Eve looked directly into Kate's eyes from her reflection. Kate smirked back.

"I was just gonna see if he agrees with you interfering in Christine's past... Yes Eve I know your sordid little secrets. You and Michael, I have got eyes and ears you know!" Kate twisted round on the small swivel stool she was sat on to look at Eve.

"What else do you think you know Kate?!" Eve asked making a grab at her hand as she pulled away.

"I don't want you to use your tricks on me Eve." She said standing up. Eve walked up to her, leaving an inch between them.

You have no choice." Eve said as she blinked her eyes, opening them with a glowing light, "Paralysed!" She announced as Kate found that she could no longer move.

Eve grabbed her arm and plugged herself into Kate. She saw Kate with Lucas, at the night club and making love next to a roaring fire. Then she had a sudden glimpse of Kate's knowledge of the truth about her mother, Sister Vern. Her anger of the knowledge gave Lucas strength over Kate. Eve then released her.

"Argh, get off me." Kate managed to pull away from Eve, her eyes filled with a black darkness. She blinked once and they were back to normal again.

"So now you know," Kate said destructively.

"Kate you can't become his pawn." Eve said.

"Pawn? I'm more free now than I have ever been and I can see my future better than ever."

"Kate this is not the way. Why don't you talk to Sister Vern, find the truth with her."

"Yes right, Vern my loving mother who left me to rot, you... you knew didn't you? From when you first saw inside me... and you said nothing!" Kate angrily insisted.

"I did what I thought was best at that moment in time. I was trying to protect you and stop Lucas ... you think telling you would have helped?"

"You could have explained later, when I was piecing my life back together." Kate insisted as she walked passed Eve into the living area.

"Just to announce to you all, I'm leaving... I know Sister Vern's my mother, who doesn't give a shit and she knew all along!" Kate pointed her finger at Eve as she ran up the metal stairs.

"Hey, wait!" Darrel shouted jumping up from the sofa.

"Leave it Darrel, she has made her choice" Eve said grabbing his arm.

"Went well then... What you going to say to Martin?" Astra asked.

"I will tell Martin and Father Josh the truth. Oh and just to let you all know, Kate has been working with Lucas... I saw it for myself."

"Well we thought that's why she's been acting strange. What about Sister Vern, did you know all the time?" Darrel asked, worried what Kate might have brought upon them.

"I'll have to explain things to Father Josh about Kate and Lucas... I knew about Sister Vern and Kate for a while, just wish Vern had told her." Eve explained dreading the phone call she was about to make.

Eve put down the phone and looked at the others as they searched her with their eyes for answers.

Jin-Joel looked directly at Eve as she spoke.

"Father Josh and Sister Vern are coming over; they will catch a flight tomorrow morning. I'll explain to them about Michael then." Eve reassured them all.

"As soon as Michael rings, find out if he's ok, I need to know where he is. Lucas knows about him." Eve told the others with urgency in her voice.

"Ok, that's a definite." Darrel said.

"I'm going with Jin-Joel to see if there is any trace of Kate." Astra said.

"Take your mobile and be careful." Darrel nodded at Jin-Joel to say 'see you soon'.

"We will stay in case Kate comes back." Eve said to Darrel and the others.

While waiting patiently, thoughts drowned Darrel's mind of what Kate had said to them all. Maybe Eve did hide things from them but it was for a good reason at the time.

Eve was in a meditative state when the phone began to ring upstairs.

"Phone! Eve, phone... I think it's Michael." Darrel said placing his hand over the receiver.

Eve took the phone and a deep breath, she really did not want to be telling him to hide, to run even, in case Kate had already got to Lucas.

"Michael, hi."

"Mum... Eve, sorry wasn't thinking, we are ok. Dad is going for a drug and alcohol screening test tomorrow, he wants to prove to the social workers it's safe for me to move home." Michael sounded excited and so sure in Jake.

"Michael, that's great, great! . . . Michael we have a bit of problem." Michael and Eve hit that silence barrier, both knowing something was about to unfold.

"What's happened?" Michael asked concerned.

"Lucas knows about you... about us, and soon meeting you again might come to a head." Eve waited for a reply, but none came. "Michael, where are you now?"

"I'm waiting for dad, he is meeting me at the bank, he wants to go through some papers with the manager."

"What bank Michael?"

"London Bank. Great London Bank... near the riverside."

"I will be there in a moment, don't go anywhere else, I'll meet you inside the bank. Ok?" Eve insisted, she didn't want to take any chances.

"I understand, but what do I tell dad?" Michael sounded unsure.

"Trust me, don't tell him a thing until I get there!"

"Ok, I will see you soon then."

Eve dragged on her boots in a hurry, "I need to borrow the Civic, and meet Michael."

"Eve, you'll be better off running to the bank from here, you'll be there much quicker." Darrel suggested.

Eve looked at her watch, it read 2pm.

"You're right, stay here Darrel, I won't be long."

Eve ran from the front doors towards the left. She ran down Ludgate Hill towards Queen Victoria Street. All she could think of was keeping her friends from harm.

Pushing through the crowds of people she eventually made it to the bank. She caught her breath outside, and as she did her senses picked up something happening inside the bank. It wasn't Lucas, it was something else. Eve closed her eyes and felt a strong breeze on her face. 'Robbery,' she said to herself as flashing pictures in her head introduced two masked men with shot-guns to her. She opened her eyes and quickly looked around. There it was, a bright red Mondeo sat humming by the tube

station with a blonde haired man staring into the rear view mirror and tapping his fingers on the steering wheel.
She caught her breath and stood up straight, she brushed her hair back from her shoulders and walked towards the waiting red Mondeo. She took a woman's unlit cigarette from her mouth as she went to light it, "Hey!" the woman shouted, but Eve walked on towards the red car. She ignored the woman and watched the man behind the steering wheel watching her walk towards him in his side view mirror.
"Hi," she said.
"Hi," the blonde man said unsure of what was to come next.
"You got a light?" Eve asked leaning against his door and placing the cigarette towards her lips.
"Yer, sure," he said with a slight frigidness to his voice, reaching over to a green clipper in the centre console of the car. As he moved, so did Eve, she placed her hand in the car and switched off the engine, taking the keys.
"What do you think you are doing?" the man said as he swiftly turned back towards her.
"Stopping you, from what you're about to do," Eve answered punching him square in the side of his head, knocking him unconscious.
She stood up and looked around, and then headed towards the bank once more and went back passed the woman who she had taken the cigarette from, "Here, this is yours. Sorry about that, I'll let you finish killing yourself now!" She mocked at her.
"Yer, thanks!" The woman stood with her mouth open looking at the man in the Mondeo, a bit disturbed by what Eve had just done.
"Hey you got a mobile on you?" Eve asked a young man wearing a grey fitted suit.
"Er, yer, sure, what do you want it for?" he asked worried he was going to be robbed.
"Ring the police, tell them there are two men in the London Bank about to rob it and the get-away driver has parked by the underground just there." Eve pointed and dropped the keys to the Mondeo in the man's hand.
"I'm not sure I should get involved." The man said.
Eve placed her hand on his shoulder and whispered in his ear, "Just ring them now." The man nodded and started to dial the number as Eve approached the doors of the bank.

It was like slow motion in a movie when Eve entered the bank. She pushed both glass doors open at the same time and walked through as the breeze blew her hair away from her shoulders. Eve's jacket blew open and revealed she was carrying a weapon, her sword. She looked around instantly; the seven cashiers' windows were to her left along the wall of the corridor. There were cash machines 30ft in front of her and at least 20 people lay scattered on the floor with their bellies to the floor and their hands on their heads.

The two gunmen were at the sixth cashier window, one had his gun pointing down through the hole in the bottom of the window, waiting for any deliverance and the other faced the scattered people lying on the hard carpeted floor. He turned and faced Eve.

Eve could see Michael and Jake beside each other on the floor about 10ft in front of the gunmen. There was an old lady next to Michael on his right.

"Hey you!" the man shouted towards Eve, "You place the chain through the door handles, then lay on the floor," he demanded.

Michael raised his head and saw Eve, "Dad it's Eve," he whispered.

Eve placed the chain through the handles as instructed then turned around to face the gunman again.

"No talking boy!" The gunman shouted at Michael.

As Eve turned the gunman caught a glimpse of her sword under her jacket.

"What's this, a hero? Drop you weapon!"

Eve looked toward her sword and with her head still tilted down, she looked up at him. "No!" Was her simple reply. The man seemed shocked and started to walk over to the old woman, he placed a gun near her head.

"I said drop your weapon!" he demanded.

"And I said NO!"

The second gunman still pointed his gun at the woman behind the desk, but pulled out a handgun from his trousers too. He turned his face and his handgun at Eve.

"Do as he says, or you will be the first victim!" he insisted.

Eve closed her eyes and filled herself with light, she looked at the two men and her eyes blazed.

"No one will be your victim," she replied in that echoed eerie tone.

Scared and shocked the gunman at the window shot one bullet towards her and people started to freak out and scream about the gun going off.

Light blazed around Eve and the bullet entered the glowing light and simply fell to the floor.

Then by Eve taking the gunman's attention it gave the cahier enough time to hit the security switch under the counter. The steel protector barriers fell down around the cashier windows and the alarm rang out.

"What the hell are you?" The man with the handgun shouted at Eve as panic started to set in.

"Stay down!" The man with the handgun shouted at the others on the floor.

"Nathan, how do we get out of here?"

"Don't use my real name... Front door I guess. We can take a hostage..."

The younger gunman grabbed a young suited woman worker of the bank by the arm.

"Get up," he demanded.

"W-w-what you going to do to me?" she replied, clearly in fear.

"Nothing if you do what we ask," he replied dragging her closer toward his chest and placing an arm around her neck.

Eve looked on at them knowing soon the police would be there.

"Move out of the way!" Nathan demanded as he approached Eve waving his handgun around.

Eve walked towards him and they met in the middle of the bank, face to face.

"You're not leaving," she insisted.

"Out of the way now or I will really hurt you," he claimed as he went to push into Eve.

Eve closed her eyes in a split-second; she puckered up her lips and gave a sudden blow of air on his face and light sparked around his head.

"What have you done?!" Nathan asked as he stumbled around dizzy, then he collapsed on to the floor. Eve kicked away his guns towards Jake.

"W-w-what did you do?" asked the younger panic-stricken gunman holding the young women firmly.

"A party trick," Eve answered.

The young blonde bank workers' eyes filled with tears.

"Please let me go," she pleaded.

Eve could sense the girl was not alone in her presence; she also carried another life inside her.

"Let her go!" Eve demanded.

"No!" Came the reply.

He walked passed Eve with his gun pointed at the girl the whole time, and then he turned his back to the front doors.

'BANG!' came a single shot from outside the bank. Glass shattered behind the gunman's back, his eyes filled with instant pain. As blood spurted from the back of his shoulder, pain also hit the blonde girls' face as the bullet planted itself in between her back and chest.

Both of them dropped to the floor and more screams filled the air.

"Move away from the doors," came a man's echoed voice from outside. Eve ran over to the door and pulled the gunman away from the girl.

"Please, I can't breathe, I'm pregnant... my baby," cried the girl. As Eve took her hand away from her back, it was covered in blood.

"You're not going anywhere." Eve told her.

"What's your name?" Eve asked.

"Suzie."

"Well Suzie, I have a bag full of tricks today." Eve tried to make her smile as the people started to get up and squirm into themselves.

"Can you help her?" Jake asked Eve, placing his hand on her back as she crouched on the floor beside Suzie.

The armed police units made their way inside and some of the witnesses shouted at them, pointing towards the two gunmen on the floor. One lady cried and shouted to one of the police officers pointing him in the direction of Eve and the blonde girl that lay bleeding on the floor.

"They have taken down a young woman over here!" One of the officers shouted making his way over to Eve.

"No! You did this to her" Jake stood up and raised his voice as officers started to escort people out of the doors.

"Medic, we need a Paramedic over here!" The police officer shouted on his radio as Eve closed her eyes and placed a hand on Suzie's chest and another on her stomach. Eve could feel the two lives she held in life's balance, Eve filled herself with white light and it poured itself into Suzie too. Eve breathed in as Suzie gasped, her wound and spilt blood blazed with light and her body filled itself with the healing energy. Suzie's eyes burned like Eves as Eve took her hands away. Suzie smiled up at her.

"You're her aren't you? The women on the TV from the news report of the cemetery." Suzie took quick breaths.

"Calm down, try not to talk." Eve insisted in a soft voice as a paramedic quickly took over and placed Suzie on to a trolley.

Suzie's hand slipped away from Eves as she was wheeled away.

"Look!" said Michael picking up the bullet that had hit Suzie from the floor.

"You healed her didn't you?" Jake said as he felt a warm glow inside and the hairs pricked up on the back of his neck.

"Jake, Michael, we really need to leave now. Jake I need to tell you something." Eve insisted as they stepped into the line of police.

Eve tried to mingle them through the crowd of people desperately trying for them all not to be spotted.

"I will get you, BITCH!" a muffled voice shouted out from behind them as they made a dash out of the way.

The three men who had plotted the bank robbery where being placed in a big white police van as Eve, Jake and Michael ran down the street.

"I can't believe this, its all true, everything Michael told me is true." Jake stopped walking and Eve turned towards him.

"Chrissy, sorry I mean Eve, I am so sorry for not trusting in you. Michael I am sorry I should have believed you." Jake placed a hand on Michaels face and rubbed his thumb on his cheek reassuringly.

"Dad I have missed you so much" Michael blurted out as they both engaged in a father and son moment.

"We have to get away from here boys I really need to explain why I needed to see you so urgently. Something dark and evil is coming and you both need to know what it is." Eve lowered her eyes and a chill ran down her spine as the breeze picked up. "You know I am of light and good and a protector of all, but there is also darkness and things of evil that exist on this land, things that you can't see or sense that watch us all the time. You need to be aware Lucas is on a warpath more than ever and his darkness and creatures of destruction will try to find you and will use you anyway they can. You need to be careful and you need to stay safe."

WHISPERS AND SECRETS

Kate watched the people's faces coming and going as she sat on a bench against a wall facing the tube.

People rushed from a tube train to the stairs, to catch the next tube they needed.

Kate looked at her watch as another tube train left for Victoria station. The light flickered in the station and a breeze caught her hair. She felt Lucas approaching and searched around with her eyes. As she looked to her left she heard a voice.

"Kate, you wanted to see me, I heard your voice calling out," he said as she spun her head round towards him. He sat down next to her.

"Lucas, it's all coming as you said it would, I have found Eve's weakness. She has been seeing her son, from her previous life."

Lucas touched her hand and smiled, "What's his name?"

"Michael."

Lucas stood up and his long black jacket whipped around him.

"I will see the Spiritual Council... Come!" he said promptly as four dark figures stepped out from the shadows on the wall behind him. Kate gasped slightly as the dark figures had startled her. They walked behind Lucas and stopped as he did.

"Come!" he ordered Kate. Her body stood up from the bench without her control.

Lucas jumped down on to the track as people gasped in horror.

"You'll be killed," shouted a young woman as a train approached. The dark figures followed him on to the track and Kate swallowed hard and her pulse raced as she too jumped down on to the track.

They all walked into the shadows of the tunnel in front of them. As Lucas hit the shadows he disappeared and so did the dark figures. The train raced up behind them as Kate closed her eyes and stepped into the tunnel.

The air was silent; she could only see darkness in front of her as she walked on. No noise whatsoever, the echoes of the station had stopped. The only noise she heard was the ringing in her ears. Her breathing started to become heavy, she blinked her eyes and suddenly as she opened them she was in a dimly lit old stone room. Lucas stood in front of her. In between them both seemed to be some sort of black stone font. The room was lit by candles, the four figures stood round the font, two each side in between Lucas and Kate.

Kate looked into the font as a green swirling mass of energy circled inside. She realised she had entered a realm of darkness and a cold disturbing feeling sunk down in her stomach. This was Lucas's dwelling and now she was part of it.

Lucas looked at Kate's dimly lit face over the font; he then closed his eyes and talked into the air around them.

"Estee Mon-greck Calabram, Council of the heavens I ask of your presence. In my questions I ask of you to bear witness. Please enter and answer my calling. Estee Mon-greck Calabram." Lucas took a second in deep thought with his eyes still tightly closed.

Lucas opened his eyes as the candles grew into wild flames for just a second. Darkness filled his eyes and the dark smoky figures emerged into cloaked covered beings. They pulled down their hoods and a black substance dribbled from their eyes. The candles dimmed down and flickered as Kate gasped from what she had seen in front of her, she now desperately wanted to leave.

The candles glowed bright once more and Kate caught sight of the gruesome creatures' faces. They had burnt black flesh peeling from them. She tried to turn away but one of them grabbed her arm and held it over the stone font.

"What are you doing?" Kate screeched as a lump of bloody flesh fell away from the creature's hand, showing part of the bones that held it together.

"Hold still!" Lucas demanded as he took a small blade from the side of the font.

"It's ok I just need a little human blood" he took hold of her hand as she pulled away in fright. Lucas looked into her and played with her mind. "I said hold still!" he shouted into her intensely.

Kate did as she was told, she was just glad Lucas held onto her now and not the gruesome creature before her.

"I ask of your presence, Estee Mon-greck Calabram."

The font started to move inside as a swirling mass of green and white light got brighter. The light smoked away and slowly crept up the inside of the font, Lucas pierced Kate's left index finger and blood splashed into the swirling mass.

A booming voice sounded in the room as the light beamed up out of the font, to reveal a graceful mans face.

"I am Jehudiel, Archangel of liaisons between the Lord of Light and man."

"Jehudiel, go and tell your Lord and father, I have found Eves weakness. She had a son in her past life and I am sure she wouldn't want him to come to any harm. Christine Clover was her name and Michael was her son. So now I know."

"Lucas, we already know of this path between them, and Eve already knows she will have to make a choice, in her heart she has already chosen. The Lord has already decided to let this come to pass."

"Then it will be her downfall and all of yours, as the chained and buried beasts of the fallen begin to wake." Lucas replied.

"Your powers grow weak Lucas as your father Samyaza awakes from his prison. It will soon be your judgement as well as his." Jehudiel's image and voice began to fade away.

"Arrr!" Lucas roared out as the energy from the font faded back into darkness.

"We will take Michael and see what path Eve will choose!" Lucas looked at Kate, his eyes still burned with black energy as he reached out his hands towards her face.

"Kate you will help me!" Lucas stated as he held her face in his hands. She pulled back slightly as he revealed his razor sharp teeth. Lucas then buried his lips into hers filling her with his dark energy as she struggled to breath.

Michael was sleeping on the sofa in the living area at Eves place when Father Josh and Sister Vern arrived. Jin-Joel stood at the top of the metal staircase looking down into the living area. Astra rushed Michael off to Eve's bedroom when Jin-Joel announced their arrival.

"Father Josh and Sister Vern have arrived." He spoke out confidently as they approached from behind him.

Eve gazed her eyes upon them from the bottom of the stairs.

"Do we have trouble?" Father Josh asked as he approached her.

"Just a little." She admitted as she pecked them both on the cheek.

Vern's eyes searched around the room for Kate to emerge.

"She's not here, she didn't come back." Darrel insisted and wondered what Vern could say to her anyway to make a difference to how Kate must be feeling.

"She didn't come back? Well do you know where she is? ... I should have explained things to her a long time ago. I should have told her the truth but I guess I felt ashamed." Vern said with sorrowful eyes.

"Sister Vern, we can't dwell on this now. What should have been said or done just does not matter at the moment. Kate has taken Lucas's side and probably knows more than we think. If you want her back, we are going to have to fight for her." Eve told the truth, only them all standing together would get Kate back. Eve knew in herself the time approached to finish Lucas, before the other fallen beasts awoke.

Father Josh stood firm and listened to her, proud of what she was and was still growing into. A warrior to defeat the evil and darkness.

"There's something else you both need to know. Christine's son Michael has found me and knows of what I am." Eve felt a piercing feeling as Josh's eyebrows raised in horror.

"How did this happen? If Lucas knows who you were we are all in trouble, he can use that life against you!" Father Josh tried to explain what Eve already knew.

"I have confronted the Spiritual Guides Father, I know what needs to be done." Eve tried to explain as Michael stepped from her bedroom. She felt his presence and closed her eyes, waiting for the drama to unfold. Father Josh's eyes gazed upon the young male behind Eve.

"This can't be, you brought him here?! Michael, Christine's son, your son, he will be our downfall, your downfall, you selfish child!" Father Josh filled with anger. He thought maybe he had made a terrible mistake awakening the soul before him.

"Your anger is not helping Father! Michael is here for a reason, in a way I have not yet seen, he is needed to finish this all with Lucas. I'm just not sure how." Eve searched inside herself for the reasons Michael was with her now.

Father Josh got closer to Eve, "I hope you're right," he said unsure, but willing to listen.

Michael walked over towards Astra and Darrel and Astra placed an arm around his shoulders.

"It's ok," she whispered to him.

"Eve, I will leave you all to talk, I have to sort out stuff at the care home anyway." He softly smiled at Eve as she turned to face him.

"Ok Michael, be careful."

"I will," he said lowering his eyes before Father Josh and Sister Vern as he ran up the stairs towards Jin-Joel.

"At least he speaks your name." Father Josh admitted surprised.

"What did you expect, he knows she is not Christine, she told him the truth." Sister Vern said with regret in her voice, wishing she had done the same with Kate many years ago. "I'm sorry this is a lot for me to take in." Sister Vern sat down on the sofa with her hands and fingers crossed together in front of her, looked almost like she was praying.

"We will find Kate, Vern. Don't worry!" Astra told her.

IT ALWAYS GETS WORSE,
BEFORE IT GETS BETTER

Michael stood in his room facing his bed; he was packing clothes and personal bits into a big duffel bag that lay in front of him.

"Are you going somewhere?" Came a girl's voice from behind him. Michael turned his head to see his friend Sarah standing in the doorway beside him. Her long blonde hair was up on the top of her head in a ponytail. She crossed her arms on her slender body and her blue eyes looked sad on her pretty teenage face.

"I'm going to stay at my dads for a few more days." Michael smiled back at her.

"Are you sure that's a good idea? You sure that's what you want Michael? What if he starts acting all crazy again?" She sounded very concerned about what Michael was planning. Sarah stepped into the room and moved closer to Michael.

"Yes it is what I want, you know that Sarah. I don't want you to worry about me, he won't go all crazy again" Michael explained wobbling his eyes around with a funny face mocking her and the situation. Sarah gave a big cheesy grin and tried not to laugh.

"I have a good feeling this time Sarah. Please don't worry I'm a big boy now... ha, ha." Michael turned around to face her properly and gave her a hug.

"I will miss you weirdo." She giggled in his ear.

"Will miss you too freak." He smiled back.

A tall dark skin toned man, aged around 35 walked up behind Sarah. "Michael, you have a phone call. Sorry forgot to ask who was calling." He said in a calm manner.

The man was Michael's social worker and carer Dean, he had been there for Michael ever since he had been in the care home. He was a gentle natured well built man, but boy could he shout!

Michael picked up the phone in Deans office and sat on the desk in front of him. He looked at the rubber tree plant behind the door in front of him, it was so badly in need of re-potting the roots were turning into legs. It made all the kids laugh when they had to go into the office when they had got themselves into trouble.

"Hello?" Michael said in a questioning manner.

"Hi, Michael, we will pick you up outside in thirty minutes if that's ok with you?" It was Eve's voice on the phone.

"Eve, hi. I thought I was making my own way to dads?" Michael pondered on his thought for a moment. What if it wasn't Eve?

"Eve is Father Josh ok?" Michael jumped in with the question.

"Erm well, yes last time we spoke he was fine. I thought it would be better if I picked you up, we could see your dad together then... Don't worry about Father Josh next time he phones I will ask him." The voice spoke with slight confusion. Michael now knew it wasn't Eve.

"Ok see you in thirty minutes" Michael said trying to act convincing. He then placed the receiver down and pulled out a piece of paper with a phone number on it. It was the phone number for 'The Temple of Life'. He had to let the others know something was wrong and that he had been found by Lucas.

The phone was ringing at the other end.

"Hello, Temple of Life!" It sounded like Jin-Joel on the other end.

"Hi Jin-Joel it's Michael, I need you to tell Eve I need her. I think Lucas is on the way. Someone just called me pretending to be Eve, they said they would be here to pick me up soon!" Michael rushed out his words and his voice sounded quite shaky.

"Ok Michael, I will. Try not to worry. I will get..." Jin-Joel's voice silenced with just a dead tone on the line, and then there was no noise at all.

"No!" Michael said out loud.

Dean walked into the office. "Is everything ok Michael?"

"Not really, the phone just went dead." Michael responded.

"Really!" said Dean picking up the receiver with his big manly hand.

"Damn phone line, must be the workman again in the next street. I will go and find out. It's been happening a lot lately!" Dean walked back towards the door stomping his feet slightly.

Just as Michael walked out of the office a thought crossed his mind. What if it wasn't the workmen? What if it was Lucas and his minions? Then they would already be here.

Michael walked fast back to his bedroom in deep thought; he grabbed his bag from the bed and walked swiftly down the corridor towards the front door. As he walked past the games room on his right he noticed the lights and TV flickering, with a high pitched buzzing sound in the air.

"Bloody workmen," cursed Sarah's voice from the room.

"Hey! Are you off now?" She asked walking over from the TV.

All that Michael could think of was that he had to get away before Lucas came. What would Lucas do to the others that lived here if he did? What would happen if he didn't?

"I'm just about to leave, yes. I just want to check on something first."
Michael said wondering into the room.
He peeped through the curtains behind the TV. He stared through the
window. There was nothing unusual outside on the street. There was not
one car he did not recognise. Michael stood back from the window with a
sigh of relief.
"Michael, what is wrong?" Sarah asked him as he turned back towards
her.
"Just me being paranoid," he insisted, "Nothing for you to worry about!"
Michael seemed to be telling himself just as much as he was telling Sarah.
He clutched the handle of his bag and made his way to the front door.
Sarah kissed him on the cheek.
"Don't worry, I'll sign you out Michael, I think Dean went to talk to the
workmen about cutting through the lines again." She looked down
towards the tiled floor.
"Thanks Sarah," said Michael opening the front door and Sarah walked
behind him as he walked out towards his mountain bike.
Michael heard a car engine running as he sat on the saddle of his bike and
rearranged his bag on to his back.
"See you soon," he said as he pushed himself off and rode across the care
homes' grass and driveway.
"See you soon!" Sarah shouted back as he disappeared behind the hedge
that separated the care home from the nosey neighbours on the right of
the home.
As Sarah turned away in thought, she heard a car engine rev up and a
screech of brakes coming from Michael's bike. She spun around and ran
towards the road. "Michael!" she puffed.

Jin-Joel walked down the metal stairs towards the living area. "Eve, I just
spoke to Michael," he said looking at her as she drank a glass of water in
the kitchen area.
Hair stood up on the back of Eve's neck and a vision flashed inside her
head of Michael screaming in pain as he was strung up covered in blood.
She dropped the glass of water and everyone turned towards her.
"Grab weapons! Darrel get the Honda out and be ready, it has begun!"
Eve studied all of them staring at her, in complete darkness of what she
had just seen.
"Eve," said Jin-Joel out loud, trying to get her to explain what she had
seen.

"Jin-Joel, Lucas wants Michael. He wants a fight, he thinks this will end my days here to taunt me with Christine's life. He wants to provoke a darker side in me." Eve looked at Father Josh as he stood, deep in thought.

"Do you think this should be done now? Your judgement may not be clear!" Father Josh looked sternly at Eve and the others trying to make them understand what they already knew. This was a trap but Eve would still go.

"Father, my judgement has always stayed focused. I must stop the evil that dwells here before all the light has gone. I have to protect what is good. It is you who is not focused. You can't run from what is to come." Eve spoke the truth and her belief was strong. Father Josh lowered his head and then looked at them all once more.

"You're right it has already begun. You must do what you feel is right." Father Josh smiled at this strong weapon of light before him. He felt a warm comfort inside knowing she was in control.

"Lets get moving." Astra said springing to her feet.

"I want to come with you; I can be some help with Kate." Sister Vern announced.

Eve checked her sword and placed it in its sleeve on her back.

"I don't think it would be a good idea that you should come with us, but if you feel you need to, then you will have to follow in the cruiser and keep out of the way." Eve said to Sister Vern as she walked quickly up the stair case.

Eve placed black fingerless leather gloves on her hands as they drove towards the care home where Michael lived.

Darrel's mobile phone rang beside him as Eve adjusted her black leather boots.

Eve picked up the phone. "Jake, I'm on my way to Michael now!"

Eve could already feel what was wrong and what Jake was going to say next.

"He is not here at the care home. Dean, his social worker rang me and told me he had been taken by someone in a white Audi estate. Eve what should I do? The police are involved!" Jake sounded concerned and scared for Michael. For a few minutes shock made him realise the reality of what was happening.

"Wait there, I will be with you soon. Tell the police that you have got some friends to try and find Michael too, that way they will let us speak to

any witnesses. Jake, after the care home we will go hunting. Lucas will die
by my hand tonight." Eve put down the phone as they entered the street
of the care home.
The others could feel her power all around them. An electrical charge
filled the air. Eve was not happy.

A police car was already outside the care home, a big black Suzuki bike
was parked on the side of the road in front of it.
Michaels mountain bike lay half driven over and bent up on the road
outside, just 20 yards from the care home. A dark coloured duffle bag lay
open on the path with a scattering of Michael's belongings.

Eve jumped out of the car staring at Michaels belongings all over the path
and road. She sniffed the air and closed her eyes.
"They didn't leave long ago!" She announced using her little finger to
draw her hair away from her face.
"Eve!" Jake shouted as he came running out of the care home. "A young
girl called Sarah saw what happened to Michael. The police are trying to
take a statement from her but she seems too scared to talk at the
moment… You should talk to her."
"Jake take me to her." Eve said as she grabbed Jakes arm to lead the way.
They entered the care home and Eve's eyes widened to look around her
as her senses heightened. It looked like a nice and clean place to live.
A little boy of about four years of age stood in front of a doorway in the
hall. He looked sad as he looked up at Eve. The little boy tried to hide the
rest of his body behind the door frame. Eve smiled at him as Jake pushed
open the door to Dean's office where Michael had received a call from
someone or something pretending to be Eve.
As Jake pushed the door open four people could be seen. A young girl
faced the door way from behind a desk, a big dark man sat beside her. A
dark suited woman stood on the left side of the desk, writing on a note
pad. A dark suited man sat in front of them asking the young girl
questions in a calm friendly manner.
"That's… That's her. That's the woman I saw with Michael, then she
changed… She changed." Sarah shrieked and pointed towards Eve.
"You're confused and not making any sense." Jake said as he entered the
room with Eve.
Everyone turned and stared at them both. They all pondered if it was just
Sarah's mind playing tricks because of the shock.

"This is Eve. She is a friend of mine and of my late wife Christine. She wants to help find Michael." Jake said with a confident tone to his voice making sure they all understood she would never do anything to hurt Michael.

Sarah held her hands over her face and started to cry.

"Why doesn't anyone believe what I saw? Eve... You're Eve, but I saw you with Michael. I'm sure it was you I saw." Sarah blurted out.

"It wasn't me. Jake told me something had happened to Michael. Will you tell me what you saw? Please I want to help." Eve's words influenced the room. They all believed this woman could help.

The dark suited man then introduced himself to Eve by shaking her hand. "It would be great to get a better picture on Michael's life here. Anything you can do to help will be much appreciated... Erm I am Inspector Langley and this is Inspector Smith." Inspector Langley pointed his hand towards the suited woman.

"I'm pleased to meet you both. I am just here to find out who has got Michael." Eve tried to smile at Sarah who still sat in the chair behind the desk in front of them all.

Inspector Langley moved closer to Eve and Jake. "We still need a proper statement from Sarah, she has not made too much sense so far but if you think you could help Eve that would be great."

Eve turned her head towards him and smiled, he seemed like a very caring person. He had a grey head of hair and quite a lined face from smoking. Eve guessed his age at about fifty-two. She nodded to say yes as he offered his seat with a hand gesture.

"Thank you" Eve said as she sat down to face Sarah.

"Sarah look at me please." Sarah looked up at her and Eve placed her hands onto the table in front of her. "I'm not going to hurt you Sarah, I am here to help you and Michael. I promise."

Sarah trembled slightly and looked into Eves eyes. Eve used her haunting hold on her, making her feel warm and calm.

"Take my hands Sarah so we can talk and you can stay calm." Sarah slowly sat more forward, she trembled again as she slowly placed her hands in Eves.

"It's ok Sarah, Eve only wants to help." A voice came from behind them. It was Dean trying to reassure the situation.

"Okay Sarah this is going to seem strange as your mind recaps the situation, it might seem like you are there again, but you're not, remember you're here with me, safe." Eve reassured her and the others in the room

EVE: SPIRIT OF SOULS

as Jake whispered that Eve could perform a sort of hypnotic trance on people.

Sarah gasped as she saw what had just happened to Michael repeat again and Eve saw the same.

"Sarah talk to us what do you see?" Jake blurted out slightly impatient.

"I… I can see Michael leaving on his bike with his bag on his back. I heard his bike screech and skid as he rode out of sight. I ran… I ran over to see what had happened. There was a woman, a woman who looked like Eve. She had Michaels arm. I yelled out to her to let Michael go. She laughed at me. Others got out of the white estate car. Something weird then happened. I ran over to help Michael because I could see him struggling from her grip. Then two dark smoky figures emerged from nowhere and turned into men, they grabbed Michael and threw him in the car. Michael screamed out and punched the car door. I ran towards the car door and tried to open it as the women picked me up and threw me backwards. She laughed as she turned to face me, then she changed."

"What do you mean she changed?" Inspector Langley asked confused. Sarah looked directly at him frustrated.

"Her face and body changed shape, she looked like a different person, I don't know how but she did. Then I ran back here to tell Dean about what had happened."

"Well done Sarah you did great" Eve praised her.

"Not a lot makes much sense to me, what about these smoky figures? Sarah, are you sure you have not been smoking anything?" asked Inspector Smith.

"She is a good one, Sarah would not take anything like that. I am finding your rudeness very offensive." Dean stood to face them all and stared at Inspector Smith. She swallowed hard and realised that she had crossed the line.

Eve let go of Sarah's hands, and she felt much calmer. Eve's eyes still glistened with white light, nobody else had noticed but Sarah did with a slight gasp.

"Thank you Sarah" Jake said touching her on the shoulder.

"You will be ok, and so will Michael. Don't worry." Eve said as she stood to her feet.

"Please find him." Sarah said desperately.

Eve turned to face the others. "Did you get what you needed?"

"Well yes, but this changing body thing doesn't make much sense and the smoky figures?" They stared at Eve for answers.

"That's what Sarah saw!" Eve said as she smiled at Sarah then turned to leave the office. Dean and Jake walked behind Eve from the office.
"I am so sorry for this; I don't know what else to say. What can I do to help?" Dean sounded so concerned he felt it was his fault in some way.
"You stay here in case he comes back. And don't blame yourself. Things sometimes just happen that are out of our hands." Eve explained.
"What are you going to do now?" Dean asked them both.
"Find Michael!" Jake answered.
"And save the day!" came a small little voice from below them. The little four year old boy from earlier grabbed hold of Eve's hand.
"You have magic don't you?" He smiled at Eve.
"Sometimes I chase away the bad things." Eve smiled.
"We have to go I'm sorry." She said kissing his fingers.
They turned towards the front door and rushed over to the others waiting outside.
"Kate took Michael, we have to find them!" Eve looked at them all as fear for Michael rose in their eyes. They all got back in their vehicles' as Jake jumped back onto his black bike and placed his crash helmet back on his head. Vern sat down in the cruiser and Jin-Joel stared out of the window as Jake revved up the bike.
Deep thoughts shadowed Vern's thoughts as she thought of Kate and what had made her take Michael.
"Where are we heading to?" Darrel asked as they pulled away from the care home. Eve closed her eyes and searched for Michael in her thoughts. 'Where are you?' She asked herself. Then deep in the back of her mind energy pulled closer to a link. She had scattered visions of travelling though the city. She saw Michael.
'Show me where you are' she thought. A vision suddenly grabbed her and she saw though Michaels eyes. Eve saw the route they had taken as he travelled in the white Audi estate. The vision wisped though road junctions and streets until finally resting at a couple of parking spaces under some trees. The vision showed her a place she only knew too well, St Johns Church. The first meeting place for her and Lucas.
"St Johns Church, Michael is there." Eve opened her eyes and stared at Darrel.
"Lets get there than." Darrel expressed with enthusiasm as he spun the car to the left at the junction and the tyres screeched under the strain.
"Darrel I can't enter the grounds, if I do it could be dangerous and I might be left open to all sorts of darkness. You and Astra will have to try

and get inside the church while I try to get Lucas out in the open… He will know we are coming." Eve suggested as they travelled closer to their destination.

"Eve surely Lucas can't enter the grounds either?" Astra pondered on the question.

"Yes he can, he lives on pain, suffering, and lost hope. That place is filled with greed like all temples built for the power of man. He loves to dwell in that sacred dark. It keeps him alive his power becomes more intense, but Lucas grows weaker as the other demons awake."

As they parked the car a little further up the road from St Johns Astra pondered, "Eve how do we get in to that place?" She sounded concerned.

"We just walk in." Darrel said taking a breath of air.

"Just walk in?!" Astra said unconvinced that would be the best way.

A FOOTSTEP AWAY

Eve stepped from the Honda and swiped her long black coat away from her legs. She sniffed the air and walked closer to St Johns grounds. Darrel placed a gun under his jacket as he and Astra caught up behind Eve. They tried to hide from sight of the grounds coming up in front of them. Eve looked back at the Jin-Joel, Vern and Father Josh as they waited in the cruiser impatiently. She heard the roar of Jakes bike coming closer and hoped he would stay out of sight just until she knew what was on their hands.

Eve searched her feelings and sniffed the air once more. All three stood on the left side of a wall, against a tall bush in front of the grounds. The small wall was attached to the gate that led to the church's wooden doorway.

"Eve, are they still here?" Astra asked.

"I can sense that Kate is inside with four other presenses, but it is not Michael or Lucas." Eve was right; she could sense Lucas at a closer range. She could feel his presence and stare burning into the back of her head.

"Go inside and find Kate. Keep safe you two." Eve said as she spun herself around to see Lucas standing on the other side of the street. He was in a short black leather jacket and was holding a blade at Michael's throat.

"GO!" She screamed at Darrel and Astra.

"Michael." Astra gasped as she caught sight of him and Lucas standing behind them across the street.

"Come on Astra. Leave Eve we will just get in the way." Darrel grabbed hold of Astra's arm and led her towards St Johns doorway.

Eve took out her sword and threw her coat and the swords' sleeve on to the floor beside her, this would give her more speed and less weight so she could fight.

"Let him go Lucas, you don't need him." Eve sounded stern with deepness to her voice. Lucas laughed.

"Oh… have the rules changed slightly? Did I change them for you?" He asked sarcastically.

"Lucas I had already seen this coming, you're just a coward!"

"You saw this coming and you did nothing to stop it?" he said pulling Michaels hair back, making him whimper out slightly.

"I'm sorry Eve" Michael tried to speak out.

"There is no reason for you to say sorry, you just hold on." Eve looked at Lucas's eyes, they were filled with rage.

"You're going to hide behind a young boy Lucas. I didn't know you were such a coward. I thought you would have the guts to face me on your own without using someone to hide behind." Eve mocked him. Lucas gritted his teeth and looked at Michael.

"Arrr… come on then!" Lucas roared and cursed out loud as he kicked Michael into the road and started marching towards Eve.

"Go to the church." Eve shouted as Michael stood to his feet and ran towards St John's Grounds. Jake ran from the grounds and grabbed Michael.

"Eve, are you ok?" he shouted out.

"I'm fine!" She shouted back with her eyes still on her enemy.

"How sweet…" Lucas muttered so Eve could hear.

Michael and Jake ran to the church doorway.

Lucas laughed into the air and licked his lips at Eve, mocking her. He seemed like a madman.

"I've been waiting for this moment!" Lucas admitted as he stood just in front of her. He tilted his head and looked her up and down. Eve huffed as they started to circle each other, her eyes began to smoke over and become a glowing bright white light. Lucas looked intensely at her as his eyes filled with blackness and destruction.

The clouds in the sky filled with a smoky darkness as they gathered above them. A charge of white lighting cracked against the sky.

Lucas flew at Eve as she drew her sword high towards her head. Lucas jumped towards her swiping down with his sword. Eve caught his swipe easily.

Her sword charged with a blue and white electrical energy as she pushed Lucas backwards and their swords both crossed as they met.

Lucas flew backwards, but caught himself as his feet landed first on to the ground. His eyes filled with rage as he screamed into the air and ran at Eve. She stood with her right leg forward and her sword held up ready and waiting for combat.

As Lucas ran at her there was a loud chink in the air and another charge of energy ran down both blades as their swords touched.

Eve pushed Lucas back with her blade once again, but this time he held his balance and was able to counter her attack. He swiped at her stomach and she jumped back backwards to avoid what would be a devastating blow.

In the blink of an eye Eve jumped behind Lucas and swiped for his head.
He managed to duck and used his left leg to spin around, while he swiped
his right leg under Eve's feet, trying to knock her to the ground.
Eve jumped up in time to miss him knocking her down.
They faced each other and Lucas plunged his sword at Eve, she caught
the blow. Eve swiped his sword away with hers and head butted Lucas in
the face as she did. Lucas screamed out as blood ran towards his top lip.
Lucas lunged towards Eve and swiped his sword towards her face; she
met his blade with ease as he kicked out at her. Lucas's left foot made
contact with her right side.
Eve's kidney filled with pain as she fell forward and tried to catch her
breath. Eve's sword skidded out in front of her as she held her hands out
towards the floor saving herself from the fall.
Lucas lurched over the top of her ready to stab her in the back of the
head, but she rolled herself over and kicked his wrist with her left foot.
His sword flew out from his hand and clinked across the stone road
under them.
Eve swiped her right leg out, clipping Lucas's feet, making him fall to the
floor beside her. She quickly rolled away from him and then bounced to
her feet.

Thunder cracked all around in the sky above as Lucas stood to his feet
and wiped away the blood from his nose with the back of his wrist,
smearing it across his face. It dripped from his chin and on to the road.
Anger grew on his face as he stood and looked at Eve.
"You bitch; do you think this is all I have?" He smirked and raised his
hands up in front of him.
Lucas shouted out as two big swirls of flames flew out in front of him.
Eve jumped out of the way as one of the fire bombs hit the tree behind
her that rested outside St Johns Grounds. The flames hissed as the tree
rustled with the hit.
Eve shouted out with force as she pushed her hands out in front of her.
Blasts of wind shot out from her hands aimed towards Lucas. The shots
of air hit Lucas and the other fire bomb as he held his arm out in front of
him to shield himself. Lucas flew backwards into the road as the flames
of fire smashed into him. In moments Lucas stood to his feet and
brushed away the ash and burning cinders from his shoulders, arms and
legs.

"I have had enough of this!" he shouted as he looked up into the sky and roared.

He held out his arms beside him and looked up at the sky. A red aura glowed around his body until his image changed from man to beast.

Eve picked her sword up from the floor and closed her eyes. The air spun up around her, her body began to glow with a bright blue electrical energy. The electrical charge snapped and crackled all around her, the light flashed all over her body and up the swords blade.

Lucas snarled at Eve and his jaws drooled, his image was a disgusting big black beast. He had four legs, a savage dog like appearance and his body had a shine where scales armoured him. The beasts' jaws were big and angry, he snapped and growled.

Lucas reared up and galloped towards Eve, he howled out. He swiped at her with his front paws and huge black claws.

Eve shot out an electrical charge with her hands, it cracked as it made contact with Lucas and she held it on him. Lucas fell to the floor with a big thud and wailed in pain. He stood to his feet once more as Eve took away her hold on him.

Lucas snarled and looked at Eve from the corner of his eyes; he twisted to face her again and began to run towards her. He tried to jump on Eve so he could rip out her throat, but Eve held out her left arm; a force of air shot out in front of her knocking Lucas backwards towards the tree outside St Johns. The tree thudded and then the burning branches from the top descended to the ground on top of Lucas.

Lucas moaned and stood from the flames once more but in the image of a man. He walked out brushing himself down.

They both knew the only way to defeat each other would be to take off one of their heads with the swords they both held.

Lucas looked at Eve with fear and anger; he reached for his sword on the floor in front of him.

Lucas walked fast towards Eve, and as he grew closer he ran up towards her slashing his sword one way then the other. Both their swords clinked together. Lucas drew another smaller blade from his trouser belt he tried to stab Eve in the leg as she swiped her sword and cut his left arm.

Eve grabbed his right arm that held the dagger and twisted his hand around making him drop the weapon to the floor.

Grabbing his left arm that had been wounded he stepped backwards away from Eve and he ran towards St Johns.

Lucas realised he could not beat Eve; she was too quick and strong for him. He was getting weaker as his father was waking from his prison under the sands of the earth. Lucas knew it would take a bigger and more powerful demon to beat Eve or come close to it anyway.

"NO!" Eve shouted out as she moved her sword down beside her.

Could she enter the grounds of St Johns?

Lucas pushed open the wooden doors and quickly closed them behind himself as he entered the church. Eve closed her eyes and the energy of light disappeared from around her. The wind still swirled all around as she made her way to the doorway of St Johns.

Eve placed her hands on the doors and remembered the vision she had seen before when everything had seemed still fresh and new to her. She shook her head, she had to enter to protect Michael and save her friends. Eve pushed open the doors and the wind blew her hair back from her face. The doors creaked as they opened. Eve stood in the doorway looking in towards the dim light that lit the altar ahead of her.

"Eve, are you ok?" A whisper came from beside her.

The wind slammed the doors behind Eve as she turned and swiped away a red curtain to reveal Astra. Astra stepped out from the shadows as did the rest of them carrying their weapons.

Eve studied them all carefully as she nodded to Astra that she was ok.

"Where is Michael and Jake?" she asked concerned as they where not to be seen.

"When Lucas came through the door Kate stabbed Jake in the leg. Lucas grabbed Michael and ran off. Jake has gone after them both." Astra spilled out what had happened in seconds.

"Lucas we have not finished our little interlude yet!" Eve shouted out as she walked on towards the altar.

Astra walked behind her turning to look all around as she searched the shadows for any hidden surprises. Darrel stood by the doorway with Jin-Joel in a pose that said they were ready to fight.

Eve walked up the steps to the altar and held her sword tightly with both hands in front of her. Astra looked up at her as she shouted out once more.

"Jake... Michael!" Eve could sense Kate was near and she was out for blood now she had spilt Jakes.

"Looking for me?" Kate snarled at Astra and Eve as she stood from out of the shadows. Astra turned to see her stand up from the front aisle and she stood back ready to defend herself and Eve. Astra pointed her hand gun at Kate.

"What do you want Kate?" Astra stared at her face as it filled with anger.

"I want blood; I want to see you all scream in terror for hiding the truth from me. All your secrets and lies that filled my head and you all kept telling yourselves, you were keeping things from me to protect me. I WANT TO SEE YOU ALL DIE!" Kate's voice raged out as she launched her self at Astra and punched her straight in the face.

Astra stepped backwards slightly dazed and walked backwards towards the wooden benches behind her. She held her mouth then looked down at the blood in her hand.

Astra looked at Kate and provoked her with a smile. Kate screamed out as she flew at Astra mocking her. She grabbed Astra by the throat with both hands. Astra dropped her weapon as they both landed in the aisle. Kate was on top of Astra trying to strangle her. Astra grabbed her hands and tried to push her off. Eve ran over to them both and grabbed Kate by the hair, she pulled Kate completely off Astra. Kate screamed out and clawed out in front of her.

"Get off me you BITCH!" she demanded.

Astra stood to her feet coughing and clutching her throat.

"Stop this Kate" Demanded Vern seeing what had become of her daughter.

Eve let go of Kate. She huffed and looked at Vern.

"Oh mother dearest, who is so righteous with her life." Kate had a provocative smirk.

"Kate it wasn't like you think. Nobody knew about you to begin with… I was ashamed of myself, I thought I could give you up to a better life… but I couldn't so I came and found you again. I have always wanted to tell you the truth but I was afraid you would not have any respect for me any longer. Your father was a stranger on the run, he did some bad things. I was a nun and we hid him. We both fell in love… He got caught and taken back to prison and I found out I was pregnant. I had to give you up…. I am so sorry. I gave up everything to find you." Vern raised a hand up to Kate's face and tried to approach her.

"Don't you come near me!" Kate snarled then twisted herself around to face Eve. Blackness now burned in her eyes and her voice changed to a deep dark tone.

"And you Eve, you knew all along and never told me, so I thought it would be fun to tell Lucas where Christine's son was. Now you will find out what its like to have something you love and want so bad destroyed in front of you." Kate hissed and laughed out loud like she was going insane.

Astra looked at Kate and shook her head.

"Oh shut up!" Astra insisted as she punched Kate straight in the face knocking her off her feet and unconscious.

"Wow that felt so good." Astra said as she flicked out her hand, shaking out the pain from the blow.

A tall figure suddenly stepped out from another door way behind the altar. Eve could sense it was Jake.

"Eve" Jake said as he walked towards her with relief. Jake placed his hands on the tops of Eve's arms beside her.

"Lucas has taken Michael up into the bell tower he has a noose around Michael's neck and is threatening to drop him through the top window.

Darrel grabbed Jakes shoulder "Here take this."

Darrel placed a hand gun in Jakes hand "Thanks, I think."

"You do know how to use it right? Well it's fully loaded" Darrel looked at Jakes concerned face.

"Yes I know how to use one, I haven't been a completely good boy in my time, but that's another story." Jake announced in a mocking tone clutching the gun in one hand and his wounded leg with the other.

Eve placed her fingers on her lips to hush their voices. She could hear movement on the bell tower steps.

Astra looked at Jakes wound, "It's not too deep, you'll live for now you might need a couple of stitches though."

Vern crouched down over Kate as she lay in the aisle unconscious; she placed her hand on top of Kate's brow. Vern felt a strong urge to protect her now more than ever.

Rumbles and vibrations started to creep around St Johns; Eve felt a deep sinking feeling inside her.

"I should not be inside this place; my presence is disturbing the dead!" Eve shook her head it was beginning to fill with nonsense and weird distracting images.

Jin-Joel walked over towards Vern as the rumbling and tremors started to grow all around them.

A laugh came out of the darkness and the shadows began to move. Whispers and hisses could be heard as Lucas and Michael appeared at the bottom of the towers' steps. Smoky figures appeared around them. The figures began to emerge into demonic creatures. Shock and horror set in with them all as the creatures appeared from the darkness. The ugly creatures walked around the others snarling and drooling as their eyes burned red.

"Stay calm everyone and stay still. These creatures are just here to make us keep our distance from Lucas and Michael." Eve looked at each creature in turn. At first these creatures paced around them all and then in a split second they wisped back into the shadows then emerged somewhere else. Eve counted four and tried to point them out to the others.

"My god, this is surreal." Astra gasped.

Jake looked at Eve with a worrying gaze, he had never imagined anything like this.

Lucas pushed Michael in front of him with a blade to his throat once more.

"Thought I could borrow him, this time for my beasts… They get bored easily you know… You can keep what's left of him for yourselves." Lucas beamed a smile at Eve.

"You bastard let him GO!" Jake ordered as he lunged himself towards Lucas. One of the creatures that looked like a large deranged blood thirsty dog ran in between Jake and Lucas. It reared up at Jake with a blood curdling howl to warn him away.

Eve's eyes burned white until she blinked and in an instant they filled with darkness and rage.

"I am going to KILL EVERY PART OF YOU!" A deep tone filled her voice as she walked towards Lucas. She walked with confidence and she felt unchallenged of what was to come.

A beast reared up in front of her, but she made no attempt to stop walking, it savagely snapped at her as drool dripped from its jaws. Eve raised her sword and slashed the beast out of her way, slicing through its throat. Another beast then came running from behind her. Eve spun around as the beast jumped through the air heading straight towards her. She raised her hand out in front of her, she shouted out as a big rush of air and fire shot out from her. It hit the beast as it roared at her; it burst into flames then ash. The ash shimmered as it scattered to the floor. Eve looked so angry as she reached Lucas.

Lucas stepped back slightly as Eve reached him, he pressed the blade harder against Michael's throat. Lucas smirked at Jake who started to walk up behind Eve.

"Let him go" Eve's deep voice echoed

"Ha, I don't think so!" Lucas's eyes burned black as he licked the side of Michaels face.

Eve scowled at Lucas and kept her attention on him, she never looked at Michael as she plunged her sword right through Michael's abdomen.

"NO!" Jake roared behind her.

Fear and pain filled in Lucas's eyes as Michael fell to his knees. Michael felt no pain as Eve had placed her hand on Michaels shoulder to draw any pain away.

"Mum" Michael said in a breath as he lay down on the floor in shock; blood spilling from his wound.

The blade had travelled right through Michael and into Lucas. Lucas clutched his wounds and stared at the blood in his hands, it had not killed him but Eve's sword had left him wounded.

Jake ran to Michael and tore away his clothes to reveal his wound; he placed his hand onto Michael's abdomen, just under his ribs. Eve had made sure she had not hit any organ that would have been a fatal blow straight away.

Lucas held his stomach and looked up at Eve, he laughed at her.

"This won't kill me!" Lucas blurted out as he raised his sword at Eve.

"No, but you're wounded."

Lucas jumped forward at Eve knocking her backwards; she swiftly found her feet and stood on the altars' steps.

"Eve, what have you done!" Astra desperately cried out as she now stood over Michael and Jake. Everybody was shocked to see what had happened.

Lucas plunged himself towards Eve as she quickly stepped sideways out of the way and pulled her sword over her shoulder. The blade sliced Lucas's throat, he lent forward clutching at it. Blood spilled from between his fingers as he fell to his knees. Eve was tired of playing games, she was angry with herself for letting it go this far. It was time to end it.

Lucas knelt down over the altars steps as Eve raised her sword into the air. The sword charged itself with a white glow that crackled as a white electrical charge hissed up and down the blade.

"Thy shall be done!" Eve yelled as she brought the sword down toward Lucas and it took off his head.

Lucas's body glowed suddenly in a blaze of light as both his body and energy died. But then to Eve's horror he reached out a hand to Michael's foot before his energy was completely gone. Lucas's energy started to glow around Michael.

"Move him, Move!" Eve snapped at Jake, Astra and Michael. Her eyes were now normal but filled with fear.

"What have you done?" Jake grabbed hold of Eve's arm and stood to his feet, he looked angry.

"Trust me!" Eve glared at Jake.

She knelt down over Michael and placed her hands on him, one on his wound and one on his head. Eve closed her eyes and filled herself with white light. She hoped that she was not too late, and she had enough power to stop Lucas from taking over Michael.

"The other beasts have all gone. They disappeared when you killed Lucas." Darrel started to run towards Eve.

"Don't be so sure." Jin-Joel said walking up behind Darrel.

The shadows were still moving and St Johns started to tremble. Vibrations started to shake the glass in the stone window frames Eve knew they had to leave before the whole place rocked to the ground.

"Eve killed two beasts that leaves us just two more" Darrel shouted over the rumbles.

Eve's hands glowed and so did Michaels body, he gasped at the air for a few breaths until Eve opened her eyes. Michael sat up as Eve took away her hands, his wound had disappeared. Tears rose in Jakes eyes.

"I am so sorry Michael; I had to end Lucas's antics." Eve explained hugging him.

"It's ok." Michael whispered… "Arr" Michael gasped and fell backwards.

"What's wrong with him?" Astra asked.

Michael's eyes rolled and they filled with blackness.

"Eve you can save Michael from Lucas… Christine was chosen because her blood line is dated back to Christ himself…. and so of course is Michaels too." Josh placed his hand on Eves shoulder.

"You have not got long. Take Michael to Tower Hill, on top lies a sacred stone that has been blessed many years ago for sacrifices'. Place Michael there and you will have to listen inside yourself for what to do. I just hope your cries are heard to our 'Lord of Light'."

Jake grabbed Eve's hand, she touched his face.

"I have to go… Lucas is taking him over, my energy will not last long inside Michael, but while it's there it will protect him."

"I will take Michael to the car" Jake said as he picked up Michaels groaning body in his arms and raced towards St Johns doorway.

As they neared the wooden doors, St Johns began to shake again, the windows began to crack. One stain glass window shattered and glass fell to the floor.

Two beasts suddenly emerged from the shadows, growling at them all, blocking the doorway.

Eve picked up Lucas's sword from beside her. She held both swords in front of her and walked in front of Jake and Michael.

"Go out the back way" she whispered to Jake as she passed him.

Jake moved slowly backwards towards the altar.

"We can't leave Kate" Vern insisted.

"Vern… GO NOW!" Josh demanded.

"Darrel take Kate out the back" Father Josh insisted

"But…"

"No buts, just do as I ask" Father Josh ordered as he took out a sword from under his robe.

They all did as they were asked.

Astra and Jin-Joel stood either side of Eve. Father Josh walked backwards towards the rear exit keeping his eye on the beasts. He stood by the altar ready to protect the others. The beasts snarled as they saw Jake trying to leave with Michael.

"Oh no you don't!" Eve shouted out as one of the beasts tried to jump over the top of her. Eve plunged her sword up into the air; it hit the beast right in the stomach. Eve knew this would only wound it for a while, but the beasts were much weaker without Lucas.

As it fell to the floor Eves own sword held an electrical charge. She sliced through the beast's neck; the beast smouldered and then exploded into ash. The ash filled the air and settled everywhere. Astra shook ash from her hair and brushed it off her arms.

"Look alert Astra" Jin-Joel spoke from the corner of his mouth.

Eve moved closer to the other beast as it raised itself up ready to pounce. It roared at her and went to fly up at Eve to tear her to pieces with its big black claws. Eve ran at it and went to plummet her feet into its chest. The beast moved too quickly for her and jumped over the top of her.

Eve fell to the floor, but swiftly jumped back on her feet. The beast swiped at Astra and Jin-Joel, but they jumped out of the way. Astra moved backwards and aimed her gun. Jin-Joel kicked the beast in the jaw as a gunshot pierced through the air and entered its head. The beast was shocked for a second; it shook its head and stood back up.
Rage raced in the beast's blood as it looked at Astra. The beast lunged itself at Astra and Jin-Joel and as it did Eve jumped into the air.
Eve clutched both swords as she landed in between the beast and her friends and in a second she swiped the swords in opposite directions. The swords crossed at the beast's throat and its head rolled to the floor.
The beast exploded into ash.
Without a second thought Eve said, "Let's go!" She headed through the ash towards the wooden doors.

Eve ran towards the Honda Civic where Jake was laying Michael on the back seat. She jumped in the driver's side.
"I think I should drive!" Jake said, he wanted to be with his son to make sure nothing else could happen to him.
"Jake I have to do this on my own; I have to talk to the watchers. They are archangels that watch over mankind." Eve tried to explain.
"But I'm his father" Jake insisted.
"I haven't got time to argue with you Jake. This has to be done with just me!" Eve shouted and slammed the car door; she locked it and revved the engine.
Jake tried to open the door he pounded on the glass window as Eve drove away.
"You can't do this." Jake shouted out.
"This side of Tower Bridge" Jin-Joel shouted out to Eve as the car spun away.
"What's going to happen?" Astra asked Father Josh.
"Life and death" Father Josh replied.
"What do you mean life and death?" Jake asked in a hurry.
"Eve will have to make a choice to save mankind or save Michael. Her blood can purify." Father Josh explained.
They all looked at each other in terror. Jake didn't want to lose Michael or Eve.
"No, there must be another way." Jake rubbed his hands down his face.
"I have to stop her" Jake panicked and ran towards his bike.
"Is there another way?" Darrel asked Jin-Joel.

"I don't know." He answered as they all ran towards the Space Cruiser. Kate lay across the back and Vern had Kate's head resting on her legs. "I have to be there, this isn't right!" Jake shouted out as he revved up his bike.

The sky grew darker as a late autumn storm rumbled through the air. Droplets began to fall from the sky above as they all raced to be with Eve.

As Eve pulled up beside Tower Bridge she looked up at the hill. A crack of lighting raced across the sky. The rain started to fall against the car window.

Michael groaned in the back of the car and cursed words came from his mouth. Eve got out of the Honda and grabbed Michael's arms; she pulled him towards her and then lifted him from the back seat. She placed him on the ground beside the car. Eve looked at the hill, it was becoming muddy because of the rain and it would be more of a struggle to climb to the top with Michael.

Eve laid a blanket around Michael and placed her long coat on the ground. She rolled Michael onto the coat and took a rope out of the boot of the Honda. She wrapped the blanket around Michael covering his head for protection whilst they travelled.

The rain got harder and hit off Eve and Michael as she placed one end of the rope around him. Water dripped off her face and from her hair as she tied the rope up under Michael's arms.

Eve wrapped the rope around her arm and shoulder; she pulled at the rope to test the knot on Michael. She knelt down and placed Michael over her shoulder and back. She walked him to the foot of the hill and then placed him on the ground.

Eve had to move fast, the rain had made the hill so muddy she knew it would be difficult to climb without sliding.

She crouched down to her hands and knees and started to stand upright as she took the weight of Michael. She pulled on the rope as she started to stand up straighter. As she climbed up the hill all she could think of was reaching the top, as the rain splashed in her face and the darkness grew in the sky above.

Jake raced towards Tower Hill; the traffic was beginning to become more of a nightmare then ever because of the rain. As Jake turned into Upper

Thames Street, the traffic looked worse. He mounted the pavement and tried to race along the path, he knew he wasn't far from Tower Hill. As he jumped off the curb back on to the road ahead his bike slipped out from underneath him. Jake and the bike slid sideways down the road, cars came to sudden screeching, sloshing stop. He tried to hobble to his feet. As he did so he moved towards the pavement and tried to run towards Tower Bridge as people called out behind him. As he hobbled and tried to run in the rain he ignored his pain because all that went through his mind was – he could already be too late.

THY SHALL NOT BE DONE

Eve lay Michael down on the grass at the top of the hill. She untied the rope and loosened the blanket from around him.

"Michael." She whispered in his ear.

Michael's eyes opened, blackness filled them, rain slashed down on to his face as he screamed out.

"You BITCH; I should have slaughtered you all!" Michael made a grab at Eve, but she grabbed his arms and tied them together with the rope. He kicked out at her screaming as she grabbed his legs and placed them in a noose she had made with the rope.

Eve dragged Michael over to the sacred stone. She tried to lift him as he screamed at her and wriggled. She placed him on top of the flat stone at the edge of the hill.

Lightening cracked through the air and the rain now thrashed down around them.

Eve's mind filled up with thoughts, she tried to ignore her emotions. She loved Michael, he was once her son, and he came from her body when she was Christine. She felt so much fear, if she let him live she could destroy all mankind and her sacrifice would have been for nothing.

How could she defeat Lucas and Samyaza, if she couldn't even destroy Lucas because he was now taking over Michael?

Was this her judgement?

"Watchers hear me! I have to make a decision. Help me defeat Lucas and save this child. Hear me Watchers. I hail to you. I take in all the powers of the Lord."

Eve's sword began to glow beside her. She took it from its sleeve and as she did it jolted an electrical charge through her body.

Eve saw the history with the sword handed down from generation to generation. She saw the slaughter of man from the blade she held in her hands, the Lord had the Archangels sacrifice the fallen angels' children on this blade.

The Archangels came to earth many, many years ago to slaughter all that had gone bad from the fallen angels. Samyaza and the other greedy two hundred angels that had followed him to have there own fulfilment on the earth.

God had ordered the Archangels to destroy Samyaza's angels and all their offspring.

Eve saw the Knights that had carried the sword for the 'Lord of Light' from generation to generation, stopping the evil that ruled the land.

Now it lay in Eve's hands and she saw the fights she had taken against the demons fury.

It now all made sense this time was always meant to come to show how much her will was to protect the good on this earth.

She would have to make a sacrifice once more.

To save Michael, Eve would have to give him pure life force, but to save the earth and kill Lucas, she would have to sacrifice what she was once upon a time.

The flat chunky stone glistened in the rain when the lightening cracked in the sky above.

Eve bent down and kissed Michaels cheek. "I'm Sorry" she said out loud as she knocked him unconscious with the handle of her sword against his temple.

Michael lay with his eyes closed and his mouth open like he was going to scream at her. The rain whipped across Eves face as a strong wind began to blow.

She held her sword into the air and white light grew around her. The sword charged with an electrical energy and the blade sparked. Eve closed her glowing white eyes and plunged the sword downwards.

"Help ME!" she screamed into the night sky.

Jake tried to grab at the hill as he fell in the rain. He got to his feet and started to climb, mud slipped through his fingers and he slid all over the mud with his feet. As he got to the top he was breathless and hot. Rain ran into his eyes and he could barely see in front of him. He grabbed at the grass and soil trying to pull himself up on the top of Tower Hill.

Thunder pounded all around as he saw Michael laying on the flat stone. Eve stood above him with her sword in the air. The sword sparked with electric as she plunged it down towards Michael.

"Help ME!" Eve screamed into the night.

Eve screamed out in pain as she also caught a glimpse of Jake.

"NO!" Jake shouted as he stood at the top of the hill reaching out to Eve.

Was it all too late?

TO BE CONTINUED...

Printed in the United Kingdom
by Lightning Source UK Ltd.
135339UK00001B/70-78/P

9 781845 493516